Dirty Ruck

Ruck Boys
Book 5

Maggie Alabaster

Chapter One

Chelsea

The roar of blood rushing through my ears was loud and rapid.

Thud.

Thud.

Thud.

Underneath me the ground was cold and hard. I lay with my arm over Sadie, my head down, eyes closed.

I waited for the second shot to come. Braced myself for it.

Gradually, the pounding receded, the sound of my heartbeat replaced by shouting. Then the gradual realisation a second shot might not come.

"Sadie?" I opened my eyes and looked into her face.

She stared back at me, unmoving.

Shit.

She was... My heart started to sink. Not Sadie. She couldn't be gone.

Nonononono.

A moan slipped from between her lips. She blinked and grimaced. "I'm okay. I think."

Thank fuck.

"But the blood?" I saw it right before we hit the ground. Hadn't I?

We were enjoying coffee and a chat, then the gun shot rang out. I'd dragged us both to the ground, hitting hard, but shielded somewhat by the heavy table.

"My shoulder hurts like a bitch," she groaned.

I raised my head and glanced around, before looking back at her. Her pale blue mohair jumper was flecked with blood. Everywhere but her shoulder, which was saturated.

Torn wool surrounded a wound that was little more than a nasty graze.

Thank fuck. Again.

"It's not too bad," I said. "You got lucky. We need to get you out of here and fix you up."

I got luckier. If she hadn't leaned forward when she did, I would have been the one with the bullet hole. Right through my heart. I tried not to think about it too hard. If I did, I might freak the fuck out.

"Are you two okay?" One of the café staff knelt beside us, expression concerned, gaze darting left and right.

"We're fine." I pushed myself up until I was sitting and grabbed a clean napkin from the table to press against Sadie's wound. "Did—"

Before I could say more, Frost and Dallas pushed through the gathered crowds.

"Chelsea!" Frost's eyes were wide with fear and worry as he elbowed through to get to us.

"We're fine," I said. "How did you..."

"We weren't far away." Dallas crouched beside us. "Ramsey and Jay went after the asshole."

"They won't get far." Frost's expression was dark with fury. He looked ready to tear them apart with his bare hands.

I'd never seen him look so angry. Or angry at all. Any other time, the way his eyes flashed would have been hot. Right now, with my heart still racing, hands damp, I wanted to get out of here. I'd come way too close to dying today.

Sadie could have died.

"Who did this?" Dallas asked. "I should have been here to—" He shook his head. He looked ready to give up playing football and become my full-time bodyguard. He was already attached to me. If I was dead, he'd be devastated.

The other guys would be too, but if anything happened to me, he'd lose it. And vice versa.

I shook my head. "That's what I'd like to know. We need to get out of here. I want to get Sadie patched up properly."

"Sadie would like something for the pain," Sadie said. "I'll start with tequila."

"You can't have pain medication and alcohol," I told her. A fact she was well aware of, and we both knew it. Thankfully, she still had her sense of humour.

"Yes, Doctor Downer." She pouted playfully. She was smiling, but her eyes belied her pain. The glint of moisture suggested it was excruciating. She was trying very hard not to cry, or cry out.

She was tough, I had to give her that.

"Help me get her up," I said to the guys.

Dallas helped me to my feet, first before they reached down to draw her to hers.

She whimpered from the pain, but let us lead her to Frost's car, which was parked at an angle beside the curb. "Is this where you tell me I have to go to hospital?"

"My brother's place is closer," I said. "He'll have everything we need."

Right now, we'd be safer there than in a public place. We were vulnerable already. Exposed for long enough for someone to take a shot at us. It never should have happened. I wasn't going to let it happen again. From now on, I'd be on my guard at every moment. I had to, this was exactly what happened when I let it slip. I owed it to myself and the people I cared about, to be more careful.

The guys helped Sadie into the back. I slipped in beside her, so I could keep the pressure on her wound. She wasn't in danger of bleeding out, but the less blood she lost, the better. Not to mention, she could clearly use the reassurance right now. If I was honest, I'd say I needed some of that myself.

Dallas hovered near the back of the car. He frowned like he wanted to sit beside me, but there wasn't room in the back of Frost's vehicle.

Frowning deeper, he reluctantly slipped into the front passenger seat. Before he even fastened his seatbelt, he was watching out the window. If anyone approached, he'd be ready.

No one did, but we got a lot of curious looks. Of course we did. Even in Dusk Bay, people didn't get shot in broad daylight every day. Every second day, maybe, but not *every* day.

As we pulled away from the curb, I watched out the window myself. Someone tried to kill me, and I wanted to know why. Did someone want to get to my brother or someone else in my family? It wasn't unheard of, but this... It felt personal. This was about me.

They wanted me dead.

If they tried once and failed, chances were they'd try again.

"Was this something to do with the new coach?" Sadie asked. "People at the Smashers dropping like flies. First the GM, then the head coach."

"Then almost me," I whispered. "I'm so sorry I dragged you into this. If I had any idea it'd happen..." I wouldn't have stepped foot outside of Storm's apartment, much less met her out in public.

I blinked back tears that threatened to trickle down my cheeks. This was exactly why I didn't want anything to do with the *mafia shit*, as the guys called it, that went on in this city.

The deeper people became involved, the greater the chance of things like this happening. Getting involved made you enemies. Enemies that wouldn't hesitate to end you, if you didn't end them first.

It was an ongoing cycle of violence I'd wanted no part of. But now, in spite of everything, I'd been dragged back into it. Whether I liked it or not.

"Of course you didn't," she said. "No one would go anywhere if they thought someone was going to take a pot shot at them." She winced again.

"I wouldn't have suggested we get together," I agreed. "After this, you should stay away from me. At least until we know what's going on and we've dealt with it."

She looked less worried than she should. And less inclined to lay blame on me.

"How do you know it was you they were aiming at?" she asked. "I've done my share of shady shit. That was going to catch up with me at some point."

"If that's the case, they're a terrible shot," I said dryly.

"Unless it was a warning," she said.

"Warning against what?" I asked. "What are you involved in, exactly?"

I wouldn't be surprised if she was into something I wasn't aware of. She didn't tell me all of her secrets and I didn't tell her all of mine. We shared most of it, but some things were better kept to ourselves. Not to mention, someone might have hired her to carry out something she couldn't discuss. If that was the case, I wouldn't push. She'd tell me when she was allowed to. If she was.

She shrugged her uninjured shoulder. "Nothing I can think of that warrants being shot at, but some people are especially sensitive. Maybe I put too much ice in someone's drink. Or not enough."

"This would be an extreme response to something like that," I said. People had killed for less, though.

"Just a little." She nodded slowly. "It could have been worse."

"It could have been much worse." I was convinced she was dead and I was next. I'd lain on that hard ground while the time ticked away, listening for more gunshots. Waiting to feel that moment of impact before a bullet entered my body.

The guys must have reached the shooter, or scared them away before they could take another shot. That, or they thought they'd done the job they were there to do and left.

Then, of course, Sadie could have been much more badly injured. The bullet could have lodged in her shoulder, or torn it apart. She could have lost the use of it. Worse, the bullet could have passed through a vital organ.

I was grateful it was as slight as it was. Yes, it clearly hurt like hell, but she'd recover.

"Are you two all right back there?" Frost asked over his shoulder. "We're almost to Ice's place."

"We're fine," I replied. "Just a little shaken up." My heart rate was almost back to normal, but my hands were still damp with sweat. I swapped them around every couple of minutes to keep the napkin in place, while wiping the other on my leggings.

"Us too," Frost said. "Dallas, you should let Storm and Atlas know what went down."

Ever since they'd dealt with Coach Stanley, they'd been asked to deal with several other things. None of which I asked the details of. They always returned looking grim, but they didn't seem to hate each other anymore, so that was a bonus.

Wasn't it?

"I already did," Dallas said. "I sent off a text to the group chat. They'll meet us at Ice's. Ramsey and Jay too. Along with the asshole who tried to hurt Chelsea."

Keeping one hand in place, I pushed the other into my pocket and pulled out my phone. Like Dallas said, the guys caught the gunman, but didn't give any more details. I considered calling them to ask, but I'd find out soon enough.

"Soon to be *late* asshole," Frost growled. "He's going to regret the day he was born."

Between him and my brother, they'd make sure of that. I almost felt sorry for him. Almost. I mean, he did try to kill me. Sympathy can only go so far.

"Can I stab them in the shoulder?" Sadie asked. "Just so they know how it feels."

Frost flashed her a brief grin. "I'm sure we can accommodate that."

"Excellent." She returned the grin. "I look forward to it."

"It didn't know you were so bloodthirsty," I told her. She wasn't a pacifist by any means, but she usually stayed out of this kind of shit. All she wanted, usually, was to live her life. This was a side of her I hadn't seen often.

"Only when people shoot me," she said unapologetically. "To be honest, I'm surprised with myself, but here we are. I feel how I feel. You're not going to judge me for it, are you?"

"Not at all," I said. "I'll leave the infliction of pain to you and Frost. And my brother."

"And me," Dallas said. "I want to hurt them too." He seemed more than a little disturbed at his own words, but he didn't try to take them back.

I knew he was still struggling with killing India,

and his feelings about that. He'd enjoyed it, but was troubled by how much. Frost seemed to have embraced his inner darkness much more comfortably.

"Maybe you should wait and find out their reasoning before you plan where you're going to stick knives and screwdrivers," I said.

"I hadn't thought of a screwdriver," Frost said thoughtfully. "Now you mention it, I have a few ideas."

"Leave some for me," Sadie said.

I pressed my lips together and forced myself to silence. I wasn't going to judge any of them for wanting vengeance, but me? I just wanted answers.

Dusk Bay wasn't the sort of place where people shot at others for no reason. They didn't just pick up a gun and aim at me for shits and giggles. Chances were, they were paid. I wanted to know who paid them and why. Those were the people I wanted to get at.

Before they came for me again.

Chapter Two

Chelsea

"There you go." Ice finished bandaging Sadie's shoulder and gave her a gentle pat on the opposite one. "You'll have some scarring, but it shouldn't impact your ability to use your arm. Take it easy for a while."

"Thanks, doc," she said, turning to give him a smile. "That feels much better."

While he fixed up her injury, I gave her something for the pain. She looked a lot more herself than she had half an hour ago. The colour was back in her face and her smile was more genuine.

"Now, let's have a chat with our guest." Ice gestured to the stairs, where Jay and Ramsey had taken the shooter, his face covered by Jay's hoodie.

"Yes, let's." Sadie trotted down the stairs, leaving the rest of us to follow.

I walked behind my brother, Frost and Dallas on either side of me. Apparently, I had two bodyguards. Four, when Storm and Atlas appeared as we reached the workroom.

"Chelsea, what the fuck?" Storm wrapped his big arms around me and gave me a squeeze.

"I'm okay," I said, trying to breathe while he held me so tight. "No harm done to me."

"I'm fine too, thanks for asking," Sadie teased.

He nodded over my shoulder to her. "Good. If anything happens to Chelsea's best friend, this asshole would be just as fucking dead." He loosened his grip, but kept his arm around me to lead me into the workroom.

Jay and Ramsey stood to either side of the shooter, each holding one of his arms.

"Allow me." Ice unwound a set of chains from a hook on the wall and fastened them to each of the gunman's arms. When Ice stepped back, the gunman's arms were raised over his head, feet barely touching the ground.

"This feels like an episode of Scooby Doo. Shall we see who's under this mask?" Ice gripped the corner of the hoodie and turned to grin at all of us.

"I don't give a shit who it is," Storm said. "Why don't we just kill the prick and be done with it?"

"Where's the fun in that?" Ice asked. He gave a tug and the hoodie fell free.

Darkening bruises surrounded brown eyes and a surly mouth. His dark, messy hair matched his unshaven chin.

"He had an unfortunate encounter with my fist a couple of times," Jay said. "He didn't want to give up the gun."

"I can't believe I missed that," Atlas said softly. "You'll have to fill me in on the details later."

Jay flashed him a wry smile. "Happy to."

"Did this asshole tell you why he aimed a gun at our woman?" Storm stepped forward until he was almost nose to nose with the man.

"He wasn't feeling chatty," Ramsey said.

"That will change," Ice said. He stepped over closer, his hands behind his back. "You can start talking now, or we can make you talk. Let's start with your name."

The gunman stared back at them, eyes swivelling from one to the other. He pressed his lips together and looked up at the ceiling instead.

"He didn't have any ID on him," Ramsey said.

Ice nodded. "That doesn't surprise me. Is he familiar to any of you? He doesn't look familiar to me."

"I've never seen him before," I said.

"Me either," Sadie said.

Ramsey shook his head. "He's no one I know. I'm guessing he's new in town and was hired to do this one thing."

"That would be my guess too." Ice nodded to the hooker. "He probably wasn't planning to stick around long. Luckily, people like him aren't missed."

The gunman's Adam's apple bobbed.

Ice cocked his head. "I'm glad you're listening. We could make this easy on you. Tell us who you are and why you aimed a gun at my sister, and we can end this quickly."

The gunman continued to look at the ceiling.

Ice clicked his tongue. "That's unfortunate. Let it be noted that he preferred the hard way."

"If that's what he wants." Storm drew his arm back and slammed it into the gunman's stomach.

He grunted and sagged, dangling from the chains. His wrists soon reddened from the strain. Gaze still on the floor. He shook his head to himself, and let out a ragged breath or two.

Storm's punch must have hurt like a bitch.

"Sadie wanted to stab his shoulder," Frost said helpfully. Evidently, empathy wasn't in his vocabulary today either.

"With a screwdriver," Sadie said. She seemed to be looking forward to it.

I silently added her to the growing list of people who didn't give a shit if this guy was uncomfortable or not. To be honest, I might as well go ahead and add everyone else in the room.

The gunman shuddered but kept his face down.

"Is it really worth the pain?" I asked him. I didn't know why anyone would subject themselves to torture to save someone who very likely gave no shits about them. He was a tool, like a screwdriver or a knife. Why suffer for that?

"It's worth it to me," Storm said. "No one aims a gun at my woman and gets away with it. End of fucking story."

"What Storm said." Frost laced his fingers in mine and stood beside me, pressing me between him and the fullback.

"I have to agree," Atlas said. "We need to send a message to anyone who'd try to do this again. They won't get away with it."

"I think him disappearing off the face of the

planet would send a message," I said. "Without having to draw it out."

"Hey." Ice stepped over and cupped my cheeks with his hands. "He can tell us everything he wants whenever he's ready, but no one tries to hurt my sister. No one. The moment he did that, he was fucked. You're so sweet to feel bad for him." He kissed the tip of my nose.

"I don't feel bad for him, not exactly," I said slowly. "I just—"

"If you don't want to watch, you don't have to," he said. "I'm sure your men would take you back outside if that's what you need."

"I just want answers," I whispered. "He could have killed Sadie."

"He could have killed *you*," Ice whispered back. "I want answers as well. Shit like this doesn't happen without someone behind it. I want to know who."

"We can guess," Atlas said. "What I don't understand is why. If this was the work of Dominic King or Carlos Jones, why would they do that?"

I looked past my brother to the gunman, for a sign he recognised their names. There wasn't one. Either he didn't know who they were, or he had the best poker face I ever saw.

"King thinks we're working with him." Storm

frowned. "Is it possible their side doesn't realise we're faking it?"

"They better realise." Ice lowered his hands and stepped back. "They know what's going on. We've kept them informed."

"And yet—" Storm gestured at the man hanging from the chains.

"I'll get that screwdriver," Ice said.

"Wait." Ramsey's voice was low, but with urgency that made us all stop and look at him. He turned to frown at Jay. "Did you think catching this asshole was too easy?"

Jay frowned back at him. "We're fast, highly skilled footballers, but now you mention it, it did seem a bit too easy. He waited until we saw him and then took off. We chased him a couple of blocks before we caught up."

"So?" Storm asked. "He didn't know what he was doing. He wouldn't be the first amateur in this city to get in over his head." He could have been talking about himself, but he was as confident in his own abilities, as always. No one would say Storm Keller wasn't a cocky prick. Or the rest of them, for that matter.

"But you weren't there," Ramsey said slowly. "Neither was Atlas."

"If you don't get to the fucking point, you can hang by chains beside this asshole," Storm growled. He wouldn't have carried out that threat, not to Ramsey, but his patience was clearly running thin.

"The point is, Chelsea was virtually alone," Ramsey said. "With Jay and I taking off after this prick, that only left Frost and Dallas. Two are a lot easier to deal with than six."

"Three," Sadie said.

Ramsey turned to her. "You were incapacitated."

Storm's grey eyes widened and his face paled. "Are you trying to say this dickhead was a distraction?"

"He might not have been the one to pull the trigger." Ramsey shrugged. "But yes, he was there to draw us away." He ran a hand over the back of his head and let his eyes glaze, going over the afternoon's events in his head. Clearly frustrated he'd missed something that was right in front of him. Someone watching and waiting to make a move.

Instead, he'd fallen into the trap along with the rest of us. I didn't blame him, but he looked pissed off at himself.

I felt my own face pale. "Why? Why would anyone do that?"

"Any number of reasons," Ramsey said. "But I

think that's the point. Someone was trying to sepa-rate us to get to you."

If it wasn't for Storm and Frost on either side of me, I might have sat down hard on the floor. As it was, I leaned against Frost, letting him support me.

"What does anyone want with me?" I asked, my voice higher than normal.

"That's what we're going to find out," Atlas said. "We're not going to get anything useful out of him are we?" He jerked his thumb towards the man who dangled from the chains, his face half turned up towards us.

"Probably not," Ice said, his voice tight. His expression was thoughtful, but furious. He turned to the man. "Last chance."

If he looked at me that way, I would have been trembling in my shoes. My brother could be sweet and threatening at the same time, but when he was like this, he was downright dangerous. There wasn't much he wouldn't do at the best of times. Staying out of his way when he was quietly menacing was wise.

The man finally looked up. "That guy is right. I don't know anything. I was paid to stand there until they saw me, then run."

"Who paid you?" Storm asked.

"He didn't give me a name. He handed me the

money and told me where to stand. He gave me the gun, but I never used it. Don't even know how. He said I'd be paid extra the longer I distracted you. I needed the money." He sagged back down.

"What did he look like?" Atlas demanded.

"It was dark, I didn't see his face," the man said. "I swear, that's all I know."

Ice rubbed his forehead with the heel of his hand. "Someone stays with Chelsea from now on. The more of you, the better. When you play away games, she stays close to you. Don't let her out of your sight for anything except playing."

"No one is going to come after me when there's a crowd around me like that," I argued. A café was one thing. The infirmary and out on the footy field was another.

"It's that or I lock you up for your own safety," he said. He wasn't bluffing.

"We'll keep an eye on her," Frost said firmly. "No one is going near her but us, not for anything." He squeezed me tight like he'd never let me go again. If they could, they'd probably take turns handcuffing themselves to me.

Of course, I didn't like the idea someone was trying to get to me, but I didn't want to be stifled either. I was scared, but I wanted to go on living my life. I couldn't let fear keep me from that.

"If they try, they can answer to my fist," Storm growled.

Ice nodded and started to remove the chains from the man's wrists. "I'm not killing an innocent man. Not when he can be useful to us."

Chapter Three

Jay

"I feel like a fucking idiot." I looked down into my beer. Maybe drowning in there was a good idea.

"Don't," Atlas said as he slipped into the chair beside me. He put a hand on my shoulder and squeezed.

If anyone else touched me like that, I would have jerked away. Anyone but him and Chelsea. They respected my boundaries. If I was uncomfortable, they backed off. I loved them both for it.

Frost was quickly creeping into that same, comfortable space. The guy got me too, so far.

"It was a setup by people who knew what they were doing." He lowered his hand to the back of the chair. "You couldn't have known they'd pull what they pulled."

"I should have," I said. "I don't know how, but I should. There's some asshole out there who took a potshot at our woman. Instead of grabbing him, we went after the wrong guy."

I turned my face to look at him. "They're going to come again. Ramsey said so."

"Ramsey doesn't know everything." Atlas wrapped his fingers around a half-empty water bottle. "It might have been a one-off. It might not be what he said it was."

"You don't believe that," I stated. "You think someone is coming after her." I nodded upward, in the direction of Storm's apartment. He, Frost and Chelsea disappeared upstairs with Dallas and Ramsey when we arrived back in the building.

I needed a moment, so I slipped into our place. Atlas followed. I wouldn't have minded if he left me alone, but I was grateful for his presence. He was better than anyone at talking me down from the proverbial ledge.

He chewed on my statement for a few moments before responding.

"Yeah, I think Ramsey is right on that score. But if you hadn't gone after him the way you did, we wouldn't know as much as we know. Besides, if you went after the person who really shot her, they might have shot you. I'd be pissed off right now if you were dead." His tone was light, but at the same time, fully sincere.

"That makes two of us," I said with a laugh. "I'd be pissed off about it too. I'd be haunting some prick right now."

"Instead, you're here with this prick." He grinned.

I jabbed my elbow into his arm. "You're not a prick. Would I be here if you were?"

"That depends on your taste," he said. "If you have bad taste, then yeah. You would."

"Lucky I have good taste," I said.

Joking around for a few minutes was nice, but it didn't shake my frustration. We were set up, and we did exactly what they thought we'd do. I hated people pulling my strings like I was some kind of puppet. I was no one's puppet. I was Jayden fucking Lang, scrum-half for the Dusk Bay fucking Smashers. I was a badass bitch in my own right.

"If you let it eat you up, then they win," Atlas said. "This was only one play. Not the whole game."

"I can't help feeling it's past halftime," I said. "If we don't get our shit together, we'll lose."

"What the hell kind of talk is that?" He frowned at me. "Since when do we lose?"

"We've lost before." I shifted uncomfortably under his intense gaze. He always made me diamond hard, but right now I was losing myself in this stupid pity party. I knew it was dumb and pointless, but I couldn't get out of my own head.

"Look at me," he insisted. "We are not losing this. We'll keep Chelsea safe and we'll stop those assholes from muscling in on Dusk Bay, or anywhere else. They won't get past us. Our defence game is strong. Right now, the only offence they have is a stupid distraction. One we'll use to our advantage. They'll regret the day they tried to screw with us."

Like always, I couldn't quite meet his gaze, but I let his words seep into my brain and buoy my confidence.

"Yeah, they will," I said with a sharp nod. "We'll be on the lookout for them now."

Personally, I was going to be on edge and paranoid until something else happened. Which was probably what they wanted. Fuck, they were pulling my strings again.

"I know it's easy for me to say don't let it get to you, but we've got this." Atlas was a muscular god of unwavering confidence.

"I don't want to let it get to me." My frustration was rising again. I tended to fixate on things. I tried to think about *anything* else, but they stuck anyway. Usually the obsession was football, but now it was this. My brain was buzzing with it.

"I know you don't." He put his hand on my shoulder again. "What can I do?"

"Just keep being you." I leaned over to brush my mouth over his. Something I wouldn't have dared to do when we first met. He was so out of my league it wasn't funny. I never expected him to notice I existed, except as just another teammate.

But then he started talking to me. He never treated me like there was anything wrong with me. I couldn't have stopped myself from falling in love with him if I tried. Same with Chelsea.

They both saw *me*. Not the weird guy who got overwhelmed more easily than the people around me. Not the strange guy who couldn't stand the feeling of socks. The way they felt, rough against my feet, that made me want to burn every last pair of them on the face of the planet. Wearing them sucked. I only tolerated them when I had to.

This was my normal and they loved me for it.

"I think I can manage that." Atlas deepened the kiss, his tongue tasting my lips and tangling with mine. If he kept kissing me like that, I was going to lose my load in my track pants.

I managed to break off our kiss and straighten up. "You want to go upstairs?"

"Yeah, I do," he said. He grabbed my hand and tugged me towards the door like if he didn't hurry up he might implode.

Laughing, I let him pull me into the elevator. While we travelled up to the floor above, he pressed me against the side of the car, kissing me senseless. His tongue sliding in and out of my mouth like he wished it was his cock.

We staggered out of the elevator and over to the door to Storm's apartment. Atlas knocked on the door with the side of his fist until Frost finally opened it.

"You guys okay?" he asked, his gaze going from me to Atlas and back again.

"We need to move into one house." Atlas pulled me inside and closed the door behind us. He grabbed the back of Frost's head and kissed him deeply before pulling me in for another kiss.

"I couldn't agree more." Frost stepped around behind both of us and pushed us towards the living room.

Everyone else was sitting or standing, except

Storm, who was rummaging through the fridge. "Burgers will do."

"There goes the diet," Atlas said.

"Don't forget my salad," Ramsey called out to Storm.

Storm gave him a funny look, but pulled out a bunch of ingredients. "Dinner won't be long."

"Perfect," Atlas said. He pulled me over to Chelsea and pushed me to sit down beside her. "Hey, gorgeous, we didn't want to fuck without you being there."

This was new, but when he said it, I knew he was right. We'd fucked plenty of times before, but we weren't involved with her then. Doing it without her now would feel like cheating. I was many things, but a cheat wasn't one of them.

That said, I didn't mind when Atlas and Chelsea fucked without me. Sometimes being around so many others was overwhelming. Stepping aside was easier for me. I knew how Atlas felt about me. Whatever he did with her, or with Frost, wouldn't change that.

Before she could respond, Atlas knelt down in front of me. He rubbed my already hard cock with the heel of his hand, only the fabric of my pants between my erection and his skin.

"I'm going to make him hard for you so you can suck his cock," Atlas said. "And you can suck mine too."

"Can I play?" Frost crouched down on the other side of Jay.

"You will play," Storm told him. "Take out Atlas' cock."

Frost was quick to obey, pushing Atlas' track pants down until his erection sprang free.

"Suck him." It was Ramsey who spoke.

Atlas freed my aching cock from my pants before wrapping his fist around Chelsea's hair and pushing her mouth down onto me.

I moaned and half-closed my eyes at the pleasure of her hot, skilled mouth. It wasn't going to take me long to come, not the way she was going.

Atlas nodded his approval, rose to his feet and turned to face Frost.

Frost scooted over on his knees and opened his mouth, taking Atlas' cock all the way to the back of his throat.

It was Atlas' turn to moan in appreciation.

"Dallas, fuck Chelsea," Ramsey said.

"Who said you're in charge?" Storm asked him.

"We can share," Ramsey said without taking his eyes off Chelsea. Dallas moved over to her and pushed up the hem of her dress. He grabbed her G string and pulled it off before leaning her over further and pushing his fingers inside her.

She moaned around my cock. Her sucking slowed for a moment or two but she didn't break her rhythm.

With an inpatient shove, Dallas pushed his clothes out of the way and pulled his fingers out of her, replacing them with his cock.

The sight of him fucking her while she sucked me made me even harder. Add to that Frost on his knees, sucking Atlas... I'd never seen anything so erotic in my life.

I wondered what I was getting into with this family, but moments like this, I fully understood. We took care of each other. In all the ways that counted.

I glanced around at Storm and Ramsey, hoping to see them touch each other. Instead, they had their cocks in their own hands, each stroking themselves slowly while they watched the rest of us.

Dallas grunted and thrust faster as he came inside Chelsea.

I didn't want to come yet, but seeing and hearing him stole an orgasm from me. My balls tightened almost to the point of pain before exploding my cum into her mouth.

Atlas was half a heartbeat behind, pumping into Frost's mouth, fucking him until every last drop was released.

"Don't swallow yet," Storm said. "Chelsea and Frost, I want to see you kiss and share."

Chelsea straightened up as Frost scooted over to her on his knees. He pressed his mouth to her, kissing her and trickling Atlas' cum into her mouth.

She swished her jaw back and forth, savouring the taste like it was a fine wine. "So good."

"Don't swallow yet," Storm said. Cock still in hand, he walked over to her and tapped the head against her lips. When she opened up, he pumped himself harder and faster, stroking with his fist until he came. He tilted his head back and moaned long and low as he spilled his release into her mouth.

He took a couple of breaths out his nose stroking himself a few times before letting his now flaccid cock go. "Ramsey."

Ramsey seemed slightly irritated at being told what to do, but he stepped up to Chelsea as Storm moved aside. Like Storm had, he pressed his cock against Chelsea's lips until she opened for him. He pumped a couple of times, hips rocking until he also came, adding his cum to her mouthful.

When he pulled back out of her, she swished her

mouth again before pressing it back against Frost's, giving him all of our cum.

"Mmm, delicious," he said, smiling with his mouth closed.

"Can I taste?" I asked. I glanced up at Atlas as though I needed his approval.

"Give it to him," Atlas said with a nod.

Still smiling, Frost pressed his mouth to mine and trickled the delicious mouthful into my mouth. It was a lot, but it was sweet and salty and warm, all at the same time.

"Should we let him swallow it?" Storm asked, glancing sidelong at Atlas and Ramsey.

They both looked appraisingly at me.

"I think we should," Atlas agreed.

Ramsey locked his gaze on me. "Do it."

Unflinching, I swallowed deep and hard. Every single delicious drop.

"That was hot," Chelsea remarked.

"Hell yeah it was," Frost agreed. He smiled at me softly.

Yeah, he was definitely growing on me. I was here for it.

Chapter Four

Chelsea

"I think we need to reconsider that mansion," Frost said, rising to his feet. "It's going to be difficult if we're all spread out like we are right now."

"You just want to live in a mansion," I teased him lightly.

He grinned. "Yes, I do, but I also want to keep you safe. That'll be much easier behind big ass gates. Living in separate apartments, it's gonna keep getting harder. And for once, I'm not talking about my dick."

"That *would* be a change." Storm returned to the kitchen, to get back to making enough burgers and salad for all of us. "I was starting to think you don't talk about anything else."

Frost stepped over to the kitchen to help him

with dinner. "I think you're projecting. You're the one who thinks about my dick all the time."

"Keep telling yourself that," Storm said with a snort. "We all know it's you thinking about mine."

Frost held his hands up to either side, a vegetable peeler in his fingers. "I never denied that. I think about it almost as much as I think about Chelsea's pussy. Sometimes, it's a miracle I have any brain capacity left to think about anything else."

"You said it," Jay teased gently. He stepped over to help Frost with the vegetables.

"I only say what everyone else is thinking," Frost said. "I don't care if Storm believes I have a one track mind. It helped to lighten the mood." He gave Jay a wink.

"It's hard not to be in a heavy mood," Jay said. His face was down, looking towards carrots he sliced with perfect precision. They looked like something out of a restaurant or an episode of *MasterChef*.

"Jay." Atlas looked frustrated.

Jay looked up and glanced around at us. "Sorry, didn't mean to be a bummer."

"You can be a bummer as much as you want," Frost said. "We don't mind. Come to think of it, we're kinda used to it." He looked around slyly.

"If you're about to say it's because I'm a bummer..." Storm growled. He waved a spatula in Frost's direction like he might punish the other player with it.

Frost didn't stop grinning. He'd probably enjoy being spanked with the kitchen implement.

I'd happily watch. Who was I kidding? I'd even more happily take part. Maybe after we were finished eating.

"If the hat fits." Atlas smirked in Storm's direction before snagging up a piece of carrot and biting into one end.

"Fuck off," Storm said in the general direction of both guys. He shook his head and turned back to cooking the burgers. For once, he wasn't genuinely angry. If anything, he looked like he enjoyed stirring them and being stirred in return.

"It's like having a house full of brothers," Dallas remarked. He sat on the floor beside me, his head resting on my thigh. "They give each other shit, but they don't really hate each other." After a moment he added, "At least, I don't think they do. I haven't had to tell them to chill out for a while. I call that progress."

I ran the side of one finger up and down his hair.

"That's exactly what it's like. Brothers growing closer, while giving each other shit as often as they can."

As the season went on, they became closer and closer. When I first met them, Storm, Atlas and Jay hated each other. Storm and Atlas in particular, would have punched each other long before they come up with anything nice to say about each other.

Now, they'd struck up a friendship of sorts. Some kind of understanding between them that mostly kept the peace.

"It's about time," Ramsey said. He sat on an armchair, gazing in the direction of the window. He looked like he wasn't paying attention, but he heard every word. "I've been telling them for ages to get along with each other. It's taken all of this for that to happen."

He was one of the younger of the guys, but sometimes it seemed like he'd taken on the burden of being their keeper. Like somehow he was responsible for them and their safety and well-being. Presumably because of his role as a go-between, between the Brantley family and us. Or maybe he felt more mature than the rest of them. Age was just a number, after all.

"Wouldn't it be nice if that was the idea?" I mused. "If all of this was some kind of twisted plan to have you six come together." Just a plan to force them to become friends, and face their feelings towards each other. Would they have done it otherwise? I wasn't sure if they would.

"I didn't need this to come together with everyone here," Frost remarked.

Storm looked over his shoulder, rolled his eyes, but a smile tugged at the corners of his lips. "No one doubts that, bro."

"It would be nice," Ramsey said softly. "Extreme, but nice." He looked over at me, his eyes dark and troubled.

"Any theories on what happened today?" I asked. "Apart from 'someone came after me.'"

I still couldn't get my head around why. In the scheme of things, I was no one. Plenty of people in Dusk Bay were more influential, more important than I was.

"I've been thinking it over," he said slowly. "I haven't come to any conclusions. Like I said, there could be a number of reasons. We need to be care-ful, keep our eyes and ears open. Sooner or later, they'll reveal themselves. They didn't do all of that for fun."

"Are you sure?" Frost asked. "I mean, people like that might think it's funny. Fucking with us and making us twitchy. It might have been a practice run for something else."

Ramsey turned to face him. "For what?"

Frost shrugged. "I have no idea. Don't tell me it's the strangest thing you've ever heard."

"It's not," Ramsey agreed.

Dallas picked up his head. "Is that a thing? Practising on innocent people before doing something to someone else? Why would they do that?"

"They wouldn't," Ramsey said. "It's not the strangest thing I ever heard, but it doesn't seem feasible to me. Practice yes, but other people are going to behave differently. Our behaviour isn't a perfect indicator of how others might act."

"Unless it was the shooter they were testing," Frost said. "Maybe they wanted to see if he could escape through the crowds."

"Slightly more plausible, but I still don't buy it," Ramsey said. "Whatever this was, it was about us." After a moment he added, "Or Sadie."

She'd gone to stay with her parents for a few days, to get out of the city. I thought she was safe until he said that.

I sat bolt upright, almost knocking Dallas aside.

"Are you sure this isn't about her?" I asked. "What

if they wanted her to leave Dusk Bay? She might be vulnerable where she is."

"Is she?" Ramsey asked, his gaze steady on mine.

I stared back at him for a moment before sinking down to the couch again. "She shouldn't be. Her parents' place is a virtual fortress. She's safer there than she is anywhere." Unless someone staged a full on assault, then she should be fine.

"That brings it back to this being about us," he concluded. "I think Frost is right."

"Frost is always right," Frost said.

"Frost is always a smart ass," Storm said.

"Thank you for saying I'm smart." Frost blew him a kiss. "Now, what am I right about this time?"

"The mansion," Ramsey said. "All of us moving in together. As we are, we're scattered. That makes us vulnerable. Every little crack we give them, they can pry open."

"We could buy the place directly under us and put a staircase all the way through," Storm suggested.

"That would take forever," Atlas said.

"It would be epic though," Jay said. "We could put in a water-slide." He glanced over at Atlas with a smile before returning his attention to slicing cucumber.

"Definitely." Atlas nodded at him. "But construction would take months and cost a fortune. By then, it could all be too..." He pressed his lips together.

"You were going to say too late." Jay's smile was gone now. Replaced with a look of despair, bordering on fear. He tried to keep it contained, but it was still evident.

"We won't let it get too late," Atlas said. "Frost, didn't you go and look at a place?"

"I did," Frost said, suddenly looking cagey.

Storm stopped placing burgers on plates, his spatula held in the air. "Did you make an offer?"

Frost cleared his throat. "I might have. And... It might have been accepted. And... Settled. *Surprise.*" He grinned around the room, batting his eyelashes.

"When were you planning on telling me about this?" Storm demanded.

"When the time was right." Frost met his gaze, unflinching. "Apparently that time is right now. So sue me. I liked the place and figured sooner or later we'd need it. I know you like living here, but—"

"Fuck that." Storm scooped up the final burger and placed it on a plate. "I want Chelsea safe. That matters more than which four walls we're living under. When can we move in?"

Jay sighed softly.

Atlas lightly placed a hand on his shoulder. "Lucky we didn't throw the packing boxes away yet."

"Yeah," Jay said with another sigh. "I know it's the right thing to do, but I hate moving."

"We'll all help," Frost said. "It'll be done before you know it. And you know what, I don't think any of us would mind if you sat out. Right?" He looked around at us.

"Of course not," I said. "Whatever you need."

"I'm not sitting out," Jay said. "You'll put my stuff in the wrong place."

"Then we'll help you put it in the right place," Frost said. "You can pick your room, if you want. Whichever one makes you feel the most at home."

Jay slid him a grateful smile. "That'd be awesome. I don't mean to be a pain in the ass."

I pushed myself off the couch and moved to his side. "You are *not* a pain in the ass. You deserve to be happy, like the rest of us. If you need things a certain way, then that's how they'll be. Okay?"

He turned his smile on me. "Okay, thank you." He lightly kissed my mouth.

"I need to share a room with Chelsea," Dallas said, having followed me to the kitchen.

"I think we all need that." Storm started handing out plates.

I took one and started to pile vegetables beside my burger. Everything looked and smelled delicious. I loved that they all seemed to enjoy cooking and no one minded jumping in to help. Otherwise, preparing food for seven people could become a major pain in the rear.

"Luckily, the primary bedroom is big enough for a massive bed," Frost said. "We can all share if we want to and if we don't, we have room to have our own time. It's perfect, you'll see."

Chapter Five

Chelsea

"Is that the last box?" I placed it down beside the others and rubbed my back.

We'd spent the last week moving. Between that, work, games and watching our backs, we were busy. Specifically, the guys moved while watching my back. I'd spent a lot of the time unpacking, but they couldn't stop me from helping with the last load of boxes. This move was because of me. It was only right I pitched in.

"Yep." Jay placed the last box beside mine. Both of them were marked as 'kitchen.' One with glassware, another the contents of the junk drawer from Storm's apartment. "I guess that means we're in." He grabbed a knife and sliced the packing tape off the top of the glassware box.

"More or less," I agreed. "What do you think about this place?" We hadn't had much time to talk for the last couple of days. I felt as though we'd only seen each other in passing.

He shrugged and handed me the knife so I could open the other box. "It's a lot."

"Too much?" I carefully worked the knife through the tape, as though it was a scalpel and the box was a patient.

"Sometimes." He started to pull out the glasses one by one and place them in the cabinet. "But you've been amazing. Supportive, you know?"

"I try." I set the knife aside and pried the sides of the box apart. I could have lifted it above the designated junk drawer and poured the contents in. It was going to look like that in a day or two anyway. Instead, I started to arrange the drawer. It might as well be tidy for a little while. "If this is too much, I can finish up."

"I'm good." He flashed me a quick smile. "I like to put things away. I know they're in the right place then. Saves me having to move it later."

"Good point," I said. I didn't much care where things went, as long as I could find them, but I knew it was important to him. Too much clutter, and things misplaced would cause unnecessary stress.

Honestly, I had the feeling it would irritate Storm almost as much. If the seven of us were going to live together, we needed to be mindful of everyone's needs. Whether it was something big like the placement of a couch, or something relatively small like this, it all mattered. Anything that would avoid conflict later.

I wasn't sure we needed three bottle openers, but I placed them side-by-side in the drawer, along with a couple of large spoons and a cheese grater that was still in its packet.

"The place is nicely decorated," I remarked. The kitchen was all white marble, and wood with visible graining. The rest of the house was a lot of off-white with light hardwood floors.

"It's surprisingly neutral." He placed the last of the glasses in the cabinet and started to flatten the box. "I'd have thought Frost would buy somewhere with bright yellow walls or something." He sliced through the tape at the bottom of the box and tossed the knife aside again.

I laughed. "He might have, but Storm would have it painted over the it second he saw it. Or Atlas would."

"Atlas definitely would," Jay agreed. "But he might have had it painted blue."

"Are we talking bright blue or a nice, soft blue?" I finished unpacking the box and handed it to him to flatten.

He grimaced. "Probably both. Soft blue in my room and bright blue everywhere else."

"No offence to the colour blue, but it's probably better that he didn't decorate the house." Although he brought the blue sectional that now occupied one of the living spaces. In there, it was just the right pop of colour.

"What colour would you paint it?" Jay asked.

I leaned a hand on the countertop. "Something very close to this. I like understated. Give me little bits of colour here and there, and I'm happy."

"Me too." He tossed the flat cardboard down on the pile and placed his hands to either side of me, boxing me in. "Especially little bits of pink." He leaned down to capture my mouth with his. He tasted like coffee and the Vegemite sandwich he had for lunch. Warm, salty and delicious.

"I like pink," I said before kissing him back.

He slid his hands down my back and cupped my ass, before picking me up and placing me on the counter. He broke off long enough to whisper in my ear, "Can I be the first to fuck you here?"

For the last week, we'd come and gone, never

staying long enough to christen the place. That is to say, the guys ushered me out after we brought boxes here, while my brother and Ramsey went over the security system. It now had several updates, with both men declaring it to be safe here. At least as safe as anywhere could be. If they were confident, I'd try to be.

"Of course you can," I whispered. I was aware of the others moving around the house, also unpacking and joking around.

Atlas was in the nearby living room, placing his books onto shelves. We'd be in full view of him. To confirm that, I glanced to the side to see him watching us. He leaned against the wall, arms and ankles crossed, pants tented. He gave me a smile and a nod to suggest we should keep going.

Knowing we had an audience made my clit throb like crazy. I wanted Atlas to see everything. I looked back to see Jay also checking in with Atlas. Just like they didn't want to think they were going behind my back if they were together, we didn't want to do the same to Atlas.

We turned back to each other and our lips met again before he slid his hands up the back of my shirt and over my skin. He pushed the fabric off over my head before letting it drop aside.

"Cute," he remarked.

I glanced down at my bra, which was covered in tiny little pink hearts. "Sometimes a girl needs to feel extra feminine."

"Do we not make you feel feminine enough?" He pressed a finger under the strap of my bra and ran it up and down my shoulder.

"Of course you do," I said. "This is just an extra touch."

"Hmmm." He pushed the strap off my shoulder and then the other one. "It's sweet but I prefer you without one." He put his arms around me and unhooked my bra, pulling it down so my breasts fell free. "Much better."

He leaned forward to take one of my nipples between his lips and sucked gently. He cupped my other breast with his hand, palming my nipple and squeezing my sensitive flesh.

I grabbed the hem of his T-shirt and pushed it up to expose his abs. He didn't have as many tattoos as the other guys, but his body was just as chiselled, a light dusting of hair on his chest. His belly button protruded slightly, adorably. Like the rest of him, his firm skin was a lighter shade of brown, hinting at indigenous heritage.

"You're beautiful," I told him.

He went on sucking while he glanced up at me. "No, you," he said around a mouthful of nipple.

"Let's call it a tie," I said. He had to stop sucking while I pushed his shirt the rest of the way up and off. Before it hit the floor, his mouth was back on my nipple, his hand busy pulling down the front of my leggings.

"I'm too competitive to accept a tie," he said. "You're the beautiful one." He worked my leggings down my knees and pulled off one shoe, then the other, before peeling the fabric off over my feet.

"You want to get competitive, hmmm?" I pushed down the front of his track pants and boxers until his erection sprang free.

"If you want to win, you can say I have the biggest dick of any of the guys here in this house," he said.

Still keeping his distance, Atlas snorted. "Equal first." He gestured down at his groin, as if he was referring to any other cock.

"Now you want to take me on?" Jay teased.

"You're both just as amazing," I said. I hooked my thumbs into the waistband of my panties and pushed them down until my bare ass was on the cold countertop.

"It's still you." Jay placed his hands on my thighs

and parted my legs, his gaze firmly on my pussy. "Nothing is as pretty as this." He lowered his mouth to lap at my pussy before sucking my clit piercing. One of my favourite things he liked to do. It never failed to drive me crazy.

I moaned at the pure heat that coursed through me, starting at my clit and ending in my fingers and toes.

"Jay," I whispered. "I want you inside me. Now, please." If I didn't feel him sliding into me, I was going to lose my mind.

Jay straightened up and pressed his salty lips to mine. "Say that again."

"I want you inside me, please," I said again.

"Because you asked so nicely." He gripped my ass with his big hands and positioned his big cock at my entrance. With one stroke, he was all the way inside me.

"Yes, just like that," I whispered. This was exactly what the house was missing. What *I* was missing while we were busy. If I could, I'd stay like this forever, with a cock inside me. This, right here, was perfection.

"You're so fucking gorgeous," he said before sliding back and driving into me again. "So incredible."

"Harder," I begged. "Make it hurt, please."

He slid his arms under my thighs to raise my knees and drive in faster and deeper, thrusting with everything he had. Everything and more.

I tipped my head back, and spread my legs wider, letting him go deeper still, until he was hitting me all the way through, rough and painful just like I needed. Holding back nothing, giving me everything.

I held onto him with one hand, while the other rubbed my clit, pushing me closer and closer to release. "Come with me," I begged. "Come inside me."

He grunted and drove in harder still, his eyes on mine as we both came, giving in to each other and a wave of bliss that threatened to wash me away.

I didn't fight it. I let it draw me down all the way until there was nothing left but pleasure and his body against mine. Filling me with his release. Making this house a home for the first time of many.

Chapter Six

Chelsea

FROST HOVERED JUST IN MY LINE OF SIGHT, clasping and un-clasping his hands.

I leaned forward to place my coffee down on the coffee table and turned to smile at him. "You okay? You look like someone put ants in your pants."

He grinned and came to sit beside me. "It feels like it. You know how much I wanted to live in a place like this, but no one else chose it. Just me." A flicker of concern crossed his face.

"I saw it," I said, snuggling up to his side. "You know I love the place, right?"

"Yeah, but I went behind everyone's back and bought it." He draped an arm over my shoulders.

"And where would we be if you hadn't?" I asked. "Still splitting our time between two apartments, while having to watch over our shoulders whenever we stepped out the door. Here, we can walk around naked if we want to."

The massive window beside us overlooked the ocean. No one could see into it from anywhere on land. The house itself was set back from the road, so they wouldn't see us from there either. The properties to either side were likewise spaced out, giving us all privacy.

Just as well, given who our neighbours were.

"We would have found somewhere quickly," he said. "Maybe somewhere you like better than this."

I regarded him for a moment. "Is that what's bothering you? You don't think I like living here?"

"I think you like to make choices for yourself," he said slowly. "Storm didn't let you when he insisted you move in with him. And you didn't get to do that now either." He seemed irritated with himself, but he didn't need to be. He'd acted while the rest of us waited for— What? The time to be right? When would that have happened, if ever? But if he needed reassurance, I'd give that to him.

"I choose to be alive and not somewhere I can be targeted again," I said. "Right now, that's the most important thing. But—" I held up my hand before he could respond "—I love it here. I would totally have chosen this place. You did good. Correction, you did *great.*"

"You think so?" he asked. Evidently he wasn't convinced yet. "I tend to jump in with both feet and not think about the consequences until afterward. That's why I own that cottage off in the forest. It seemed like a good idea at the time." He shrugged one shoulder.

"I like it there too," I said. Especially the memories of the guys taking me there and fucking me rough and hard. "I think we should put you in charge of buying all the real estate."

His body shook slightly as he laughed. "I don't think the others would agree. I might go off and buy something they hate, like a vibrator factory."

"I don't think they'd object to you buying one of those," I said. "I certainly wouldn't. You'd probably make a shit ton of money from it."

"Probably," he agreed. "And it would be a good front for any shady shit. Who would suspect the..." He paused for dramatic effect. "*The vibrator factory?*"

It was my turn to laugh. "Not me. That'd be like suspecting suspicious goings on at an ice cream factory."

"Or with a rugby union team," he said. "On

second thoughts, scratch that. Us Smashers are about as suspicious-as-fuck as they come."

"I disagree," I said. "Remember when we first met? I thought you were a lot more innocent than you turned out to be. You could get up to all sorts of things and no one would suspect you."

"Don't say that too loud, there's probably people who still think I'm innocent," he said jokingly. "Maybe I should try harder to act the part. Who knows where it might get me?"

"Where do you want it to get you?" I asked. I leaned to the side to look at him.

"Nowhere," he said after a few moments thought. "I'm already exactly where I want to be. Right here, with you. We have a home game tomorrow night, which we're going to win. I have five... Should I call them brothers? Storm is a boyfriend and Atlas and Jay might be too, but saying boyfriends-and-the-other-guys-I-share-a-house-with is clunky as fuck."

"I think brothers works," I said. "As a blanket term. Or partners. Or people-I-care-about-but-only-want-to-sleep-with-three-of-them."

His body shook again. "That's a mouthful. And I want to sleep with four of you. For the record, I wouldn't say no to Dallas or Ramsey, but they're not into me like that. Which is totally fine with me. They can't all have impeccable taste." He sniffed as though he was some high-class gentleman from two hundred years ago.

"No they can't," I agreed. Of course, it didn't come down to taste, just preference, but we could joke around about it.

His body stiffened. "I realised something."

Alarmed, I sat up and looked at him, eyes wide. "What is it?"

"I realised I might have insulted you by suggesting they don't have the best taste," he said. His eyes were also wide, but he was trying not to smile. "Of course, they have incredible taste. The very best."

I gave him a mock dubious look and settled back against him. "We all have the best taste, that's why we're here. We were drawn together by mutual awesomeness."

"Yes, we were, and, as far as I can tell, a mutual love of cheese and orgasms." He tangled his fingers in my hair, his thumb stroking my scalp gently.

"Those are two of the best things in life," I said. "What could be better than cheese and orgasms?"

"Cheese, *football* and orgasms," he said. "With the occasional side of beer and pizza."

"And chocolate," I said. "We can't forget the chocolate."

"We definitely can't," he agreed. "That should have been on the list sooner. What was I thinking?" He slapped his spare hand to his forehead.

"You got there eventually," I said. "So, you're feeling good about tomorrow night's game? Even with the new coach?"

He sighed softly. "He's no Coach Stanley, but Coach Davis is okay. I mean, he knows his shit. He's tight with Dominic King and Otis Skinner, as far as I can tell. That was the point, right? It was why they wanted Coach Stanley gone. So they could replace him with someone they trusted."

"Exactly," I said. "I'd love to know who else is working with them, but it's not the kind of thing you can come out and ask, you know? The moment I start poking around, they'll wonder why."

"Storm would insist you don't go around asking questions," Frost said. "We're supposed to keep playing along, right?"

"For now," I agreed. "That's what I'll do. Keep my head down and stay out of sight. I just wish..."

"What do you wish?" he asked softly.

"I wish none of us was involved in any of this," I said. "I'd like a nice, quiet, boring life, where I can be busy doing my job and being with my six men. That doesn't seem like too much to ask."

"It's not too much to ask," he said. "I want the same thing. To play football and be with you."

I looked back at him when he clearly left words unsaid. "But you don't mind being dragged into some aspects of this."

"I should, but I don't," he said. "I have to admit, I was disappointed when Ice let that man go. I know he was innocent, more or less, but..."

"You wanted to have some fun with him," I finished for him. Maybe I should have been horrified, but I was used to it by now. Ice could just as easily have kept him there for a while longer to toy with him.

"Having him watched is a better idea," Frost conceded. "If he goes to the people who hired him, we'll know. If we killed him outright, we'd never get that."

"No, we wouldn't," I said. "My brother is wise once in a while." He let the man go, then contacted his partners to organise a tail. The man wouldn't be able to go to the toilet without someone knowing.

"Yeah, he is," Frost agreed. "I've never met anyone like him. He's fascinating, in a scary kind of way. I mean, I wouldn't want to be on the wrong side of him. I have a feeling it would hurt."

"It would definitely hurt," I said. "But he'd never

do anything to you. If he did, I'd deal with him. Trust me, he wouldn't want that."

"I bet you could be terrifying if you put your mind to it," Frost said. "And now, I'm turned on. Apparently I have a thing for scary people."

"Apparently I do too," I said. "Once I realised you weren't innocent, I saw how scary you could really be. The other guys too. It's kinda hot. Okay, it's very hot." After a beat, I added, "As far as I know, only Jay hasn't killed anyone. Yet."

"Yet," Frost echoed. "He would have killed that guy if he really aimed at you. When we find whoever did it, he'll probably rip his head off. If he can get there before me and everyone else, that is."

He snapped his fingers. "We could grab on to a part of him and pull in different directions. Like how they used to execute people. Or dispose of them. They'd tie a rope to an ankle or foot, and the other end to one of four horses. Then they'd ride off, tearing the victim apart." He mimed ripping a body to pieces.

I knew what the 'quartered' part of hanged, drawn and quartered meant, but he made it sound even more grisly.

"Do you have to sound like you'd enjoy that so much?" I winced.

He lowered his hands. "Sorry. I've always been fascinated with historical torture devices and shit like that. Maybe we could get our own iron maiden. I bet your brother would enjoy that."

"Do I want to know?" I asked. I probably didn't, but the question was out there now.

"It was like a suit of armour, kind of," he said. "It had metal spikes inside. The person would go in and they'd close it, so the spikes impale them all over."

I made a face. "I was right, I didn't want to know. What sort of sick, twisted person came up with that? Oh, right, someone like my brother. You're right, he would enjoy that. I'll let you have that conversation with him."

They could further bond over a mutual love of gratuitous violence.

"Maybe we can turn the basement of this place into a workroom like his," Frost mused. "We could have a bunch of mediaeval torture devices in there. You wouldn't know where I can pick up an inexpensive rack, would you? The kind you stretch people on."

"I knew that one already," I said. "But no, I don't know where you'd get one of those. That's another thing you'd have to ask my brother. Otherwise, you might have to get one made."

I didn't think it was the kind of object you could look up on the Internet and order. Although, I might be wrong there. It was, after all, the Internet. If there was a market for it, someone was ready to make it. There could be dozens of the devices all around Australia, each lovingly made by hand.

"You mean you wouldn't mind having one in the basement?" he asked.

"As long as it's soundproof, then have at it," I said.

I suspected I couldn't stop him anyway. If it wasn't here, it'd be somewhere else. Better that it be somewhere I could keep an eye on him, and the other guys if they got involved too.

"You really are the best." He kissed my hair. "I don't think any other woman would say yes to a medieval torture chamber in the basement. You know, it doesn't have to be all about torture. We could have fun down there too."

"That sounds more like my kind of thing," I said. "You might even convince me to help set it up. We could have a swing, and a wall of vibrators."

"I knew there was a reason why I bought this place." He grinned. "It's perfect for both of those things. Fun for the whole family."

Chapter Seven

Jay

The whole stadium went crazy, cheering and shouting. The noise echoed through my ears, conflicting as hell.

I loved winning but the sound was overwhelming. Overstimulating.

Music.

Shouting.

Applause.

It was a lot.

Atlas patted my shoulder and followed me as I trotted to the locker room. "Good game. You were on fire tonight."

I took a moment to grin before throwing myself down on the nearest chair and tearing at the laces on my boots. "Thanks, you too."

"Atlas is right." Dallas sat beside me and started to pull off his own boots. "You were on point."

"Thanks," I said awkwardly. I wasn't used to praise. When it came, I struggled to deal with it. Was it sincere? I always wondered, even when I had no reason to believe it wasn't. These guys especially had no reason to bullshit me.

I managed to say, "You too. That try you stopped right before the end of the first half made all the difference."

We were down at that point. If the opposition made that try, coming back would have been that much more difficult. Instead, we stopped beating ourselves up and played harder.

Dallas shrugged modestly. "It made some of the difference. You know what they say, a team is bigger than one person." Like always, he was the first one to strip off and head for the shower. He was always in a hurry to get back to Chelsea. If he could find a way to become permanently attached to her, he'd do it.

"Yeah, but sometimes it takes one person to turn the shitshow around." I yanked my boots off and grabbed the toes of my socks to pull them away from my feet. As if they were toxic, I dropped them on the floor beside my boots. Took a sigh of relief at having bare feet. Sweaty and smelly, but still bare.

"What Jay said." Storm pulled off his shirt and threw it aside. "You did good. You all did good. We're playing better than we ever have."

"Even me?" Atlas teased.

"Let's not go nuts here." Storm rolled his eyes, but he was trying not to smile. He stepped out of the rest of his clothes and grabbed a towel.

I tried to avoid looking in the direction of *his* nuts. He was an attractive man. I'd never be into him that way, but that didn't mean I couldn't look once in a while. It was hard not to; he was a chiselled, sweaty football god. Of course, everyone here was.

Everyone, as far as I was concerned, except for me. I was just Jay, no one special.

"It's too late," Frost said, breaking through my thoughts. "We're already nuts around here." He grinned and headed towards the showers, behind Storm, giving me a perfect view of his firm ass.

"He's not wrong," Atlas said. "Crazy is the word. Not in a bad way."

I didn't pretend I wasn't watching him undress. I couldn't have stopped myself if I wanted to. He was in a category all of his own, all hard muscle and firm skin, scarred here and there. Mostly, according to him, from childhood mishaps.

I believed it. We were the kind of guys trouble had a way of finding. Okay, a lot of the time we invited it in.

"Crazy as fuck," Ramsey agreed. He was keeping to himself, off to the side of the locker room. Not really looking at anyone, but always listening. Although, right now, he seemed lost in his head.

"You okay?" I asked him. We had good reason to be on edge, but he seemed particularly off kilter right now.

"Fine." He shrugged. He turned his back and finished undressing before wrapping a towel around himself and walking to the shower. He'd always been more modest than the rest of us, but more so recently. Clearly something was going on with him, but if he didn't want to open up, I wouldn't push. Not now anyway. Maybe later, when there weren't other people around.

I glanced over to see Atlas frowning at Ramsey's back.

"There's definitely something going on there," he said.

"Something to do with Chelsea?" A knot of worry rose inside me. If something was going on with him and it had the potential to impact her, then we deserved to know.

Atlas shook his head. "I don't know. I don't think so. He was like this before her, but now... I dunno, something's different. Maybe she can get him to tell her what it is."

"If anyone can, she can," I said. Ramsey was at least as obsessed with her as the rest of us were.

"Yeah." Atlas didn't seem so sure. He shook his head and said, "We should get clean too. I smell like a week old sock." He gave me one of his boyish grins that always made my heart do somersaults in my chest.

"You'd never smell like a dirty sock," I assured him.

"You say that now, but if you got close to my feet —" He leaned his palm against the wall and raised one of them towards me. He shook it, as though he intended to put his foot near my face.

I held up a hand in front of me. "Okay, okay you smell like dirty socks. I'll take your word for it." Not that he didn't have adorable feet, but I didn't need them that close to my eyes and nose.

"Spoilsport." He lowered his foot to the floor.

I snorted. "You can smell my feet and see how

you like it." I pushed myself up off the chair and finished stripping off.

"I'll pass until you've had a shower," he said.

"That's what I thought." I gave him a mock flat stare and rolled my eyes.

He grabbed a towel and flicked it at me.

I dodged to the side, evading the fabric by a couple of millimetres, my dick swinging between my thighs.

"If that's how you want to play it." I snatched up a towel and flicked it at him, catching him in the hip.

"Brat." He flicked me again, catching the side of my stomach before twisting to the side.

My next flick caught him square on his ass. "Brat and proud of it."

We went on flicking back and forth until we reached the shower cubicles. There, we stopped and elbowed each other for the last empty one.

If we were at home, we would have shared, but not here. Not where eyes were still watching and judging. Horsing around was one thing, showering together was another.

"You go first," he said finally. "You're stinkier than I am." His tone was teasing, but his eyes said he was thinking of me. He knew I had a lower tolerance level for being sweaty. I could put up with it, to an extent, but I didn't enjoy it. Not for too long. Especially not when my skin became sticky.

"Thanks," I muttered. "I'm getting gross."

He whispered, "You could never be gross." His gaze dropped from my eyes to my lips. I knew what he was thinking. If we weren't here, he'd kiss me.

If we weren't here, I'd let him.

"Neither could you," I whispered back. I headed into the cubicle just as Dallas stepped out of his, leaving it for Atlas.

I tossed the towel onto the bench just inside the door and turned on the water nice and hot, just how I liked it.

Chapter Eight

Chelsea

Doctor Stuart was tending to a player, helped by one of the physical therapists, leaving me to walk up to the infirmary alone. The stadium was buzzing with people, so I wasn't truly alone until I stepped inside.

Wherever Otis Skinner was, he wasn't in the infirmary, much to my relief. He spoke to me respectfully these days, but at the same time, often put me on edge. I suspected I did the same to him, but his façade was always cool and calm. Polite but still a mask.

I placed aside the kit I'd carried down to the field in case of emergencies, and opened the laptop to update the records on tonight's game. We'd had a few grazes and scrapes, but nothing too serious. No broken bones, no suspected concussions. Ramsey's knee was holding up.

All of that was good news, but this felt like the calm before the storm. Everything since Sadie was shot felt like that. Moving into the new house kept us busy and my mind off things, but the sense of impending... something was there. Doom, or at least a reckoning. The possibility of someone coming after us again. *Something.*

I felt like a fly right in the middle of a spider's web, waiting for the arachnid to come and strike. I couldn't even struggle. All I could do was hang on as best I could.

Fingers dancing over the keyboard, I entered the last of the details and saved the file. I was closing the laptop when the sound of footsteps echoed through the corridor outside.

My pulse immediately ratcheted up. Sweat sprang up on my palms and under my arms.

Don't be silly, I told myself. People passed by all the time. This was a busy stadium, even at night, when people moved around cleaning.

In the back of my mind, I realised no one had passed for the last ten or twenty minutes. No one stopped in. The other doctors hadn't appeared.

I was alone.

I reached for the closest object to defend myself with. The laptop. As weapons went, it wasn't much, but it was all I had for the moment. I inched around towards the treatment room. I could lock myself in there and call for help.

If this was a horror movie, I'd do something stupid like call out 'who's there?' Since it wasn't, and my life might depend on being careful and quiet, I pressed my lips together instead.

I reached around behind me with one hand, searching for the door frame, while stepping back, bit by bit. I waved my fingers back and forth. Where was it? I wasn't that far away from the doorway. Was I?

Finally, the back of my hand connected and I gripped the door frame.

My eyes on the infirmary door, I guided myself backwards, hoping whoever was approaching didn't hear the click of my heels on the floor. I moved as silently as I could but they sounded painfully loud. My heartbeat was just as deafening, thundering through my ears.

I passed the threshold into the treatment room and reached for the door handle. If I could get it closed, and duck out of sight of the small window...

The footsteps were getting heavier and quicker, whoever it was was moving faster now, as if they were in a hurry. They might pass straight on by.

My instincts told me otherwise. They were coming here.

My mouth was dry, but I forced myself to swallow.

You've got this, I told myself. *You'll be okay. You know how to look after yourself. You're Doctor Chelsea fucking Miller, remember?*

I held onto the laptop tighter, raising it as the footsteps neared.

Get the door closed, I told myself. I stepped around behind it and pushed it shut, still keeping my gaze on the doorway.

They were close now, so close I could—

"Chelsea?"

I almost threw the laptop and slammed the door before I registered it was Dallas standing in the doorway.

"Holy shit." I sagged, almost dropping the laptop on the floor. "You scared me."

"Yeah." He stepped in towards me, hands out in front of him. "I can see that. Were you going to throw that at me?" He pointed to the computer in my hand.

"I know I like it a little rough sometimes, but I've never thought of involving technology in that way before."

I managed a watery smile. "I thought you were someone else." I stepped out of the treatment room and placed the laptop on the closest desk.

He frowned. "Why are you alone? You're not supposed to be alone."

"I'm not alone now," I pointed out.

"But you were." He reached for me, pulling me into his arms. "You should have stayed downstairs and waited for one of us."

"I have a job to do," I said defensively. After a moment, I added, "There's usually someone else in here after a game."

"There wasn't," he said. "What if I was here to do something bad to you?"

I wanted to lessen the tension, so I smiled. "Aren't you? Isn't that why you came up here?"

He raised one eyebrow at me, fully aware I was pretending to misunderstand. "Yes. Lucky for both of us I got here before someone bad. But you were alone and that's not okay. I'm going to have to punish you for that."

"Promise?" I fluttered my eyelashes at him.

"Promise." He lowered his mouth to mine.

He never kissed me tentatively, and he didn't now. Rather, he kissed me like he wanted to devour me. Like if he didn't kiss me, he'd run out of oxygen and expire on the spot.

I slipped my arms around his neck and kissed him back with just as much passion and intensity. A minute ago I thought I might die, and now I was determined to live as hard as I could. Not wasting a moment.

I pulled him back to the treatment room with me. He kicked the door shut behind us. I dragged him down to the floor where we wouldn't be seen and yanked down his track pants before wrapping my mouth around his cock.

He groaned. "Fuck yeah, your mouth is so perfect. So fucking good." He closed his eyes and bucked, fucking my mouth like he'd never come before. "Chelsea..."

I cupped his balls and caressed them while sucking harder. I loved the way he groaned and writhed with every swirl of my tongue around his head. With every thrust. He made me feel powerful, in control. Everything he was feeling right now, was because of me. Because of my mouth and my hand. Because I was determined to make him feel good and give him what he needed. Just the way he needed it.

He shook his head, trying to hold himself back, but his balls clenched and and let himself go, spilling his release into my mouth. He grunted with a combination of pleasure and frustration at being done already. After a moment, he shook it off and pulled himself away from me.

He flipped me over onto my stomach on the cool tiles and shoved up my skirt before yanking my panties aside. Holding nothing back, he slapped my ass hard enough to sting.

I cried out with pain, but also perfect pleasure. I wanted more, lots more.

He gave me more. Slapping my cheek several times before switching to the other one.

"Don't. Be. Alone. Again," he said with each slap. "Do you hear me?"

"Yes, yes, yes, I hear you," I said. "Oh God, Dallas." I would happily have let him slap me a whole bunch more times, but then he was rolling me onto my back, shoving my legs apart and ramming his already-hard-again cock straight into me.

As relentlessly as he smacked me, he drew out of me and slammed back in, over and over until I was almost ready to beg him to stop. At the same time, I wanted to beg him to fuck me harder.

"Tell me," he said.

"I won't be alone again," I panted. "I deserve punishment. So much punishment."

"Yes, you do," he said, driving in harder. "You deserve all of this. You're going to get more when we get home. When I tell the others, they're going to punish you too."

"Yes, please," I said breathlessly. "I'm going to come."

"Only if I let you," he said, sounding like Storm.

I groaned. "Please let me. I can't hold myself back."

He grabbed a fistful of my hair. "You will if I tell you to."

He was absolutely glorious like this. Dominant and possessive. Hot as hell.

"I won't," I said. "Not until you tell me to." Even if I burst in the process.

He leaned down and kissed me roughly before letting my hair go and thrusting into me. "Come with me," he insisted. "Right now."

Right on cue, I came, my pussy clenching around him, muscles milking him as he came too, deep inside me, his thrusts still fast and desperate.

In that moment I felt fused together with him, lost in mutual pleasure and a distant universe. The world melted away and was gone for at least a minute or two. Until we finally sagged down together on the tiles, trying to catch our breath.

"You're everything," he whispered. "But I *am* going to tell the others."

"I didn't expect anything less," I said. I was looking forward to it.

Chapter Nine

Chelsea

"She was what?" Storm demanded, glaring at Dallas. He whipped around and stared at me. "You were *what?*"

"It wasn't that long," I argued.

I wasn't intimidated by him, and his anger was more than a bit of a turn on, but I didn't want him to be furious with me. With everything that was going on, we needed to be united. Not barking at each other.

Besides, my brother's suggestion he might lock me up wasn't an idle threat. If Ice knew, he'd lose his mind.

Between all of them, they'd take overprotective-ness to a whole new level.

"You. Were. Alone?" He placed his hands on his hips and let his jaw jut out.

I kept my hands behind my back to keep from mimicking his posture. He was in enough of a mood without thinking I was mocking him.

"It was for a handful of minutes and I was at work. Nothing happened. I was perfectly safe."

"You were going to throw a laptop at Dallas," he stated.

Frost snorted. When Storm rounded on him, he raised his hands. "What? You have to admit the idea of throwing a computer at someone is badass. It would have hurt, and given her time to run. I think it's fucking brilliant." He nodded to me.

I nodded back. "Thanks, I thought so too. Not to mention the infirmary is equipped with other kinds of weapons. I could have hit him with an IV pole."

"No thanks," Dallas said, from where he stood in the corner, leaning against the wall. "And thank you for not throwing a scalpel at my head. That could have hurt. "

"It wouldn't have hurt for long," Jay said. When we all turned to look at him, he mimed getting a knife in the forehead. He fell back against the couch cushions, legs spread, one arm flung out to the side.

For added drama, he stuck out his tongue to the side, lolling, as if people actually died like that.

"That's what I was worried about," Dallas said. "I have a feeling Chelsea knows how to throw a sharp implement."

"I did learn how," I admitted. "But I've never thrown one at a person before."

"First of all, that's hot," Frost said. "Second, there's a first time for everything."

"Yeah, but not my head." Dallas placed his hand over his forehead as if to protect himself from the imminent danger of flying objects.

"I think you're all missing the point." Storm glared at them.

"So to speak," Frost interjected. He grinned when Storm raised his eyebrows at him to stop joking around.

"The point is," Storm continued, "Chelsea was alone and she's not supposed to be alone." He turned back to me. "You should have waited downstairs for one of us. We could have stayed with you. We would have taken turns showering."

"She could have shared my shower," Frost said.

"Or mine," Storm said. "The point is, you put yourself at risk and something could have happened to you. It didn't, but what about the next time? Or the time after that?" He lowered his hands to his sides, but his body was still rigid.

"It's not like I went off alone," I said. "I was at work, in a busy place. You know there's usually other people there. What was I supposed to do? It would have looked strange if I went back downstairs again. Doctor Stuart and Skinner had things under control. I couldn't insist on helping when they didn't need it. I had a job to do and I did it." I wasn't going to apologise for it. Not when behaving differently might have cast suspicion on me.

"I don't care if you have to hide out in the locker room, or shower with one of us," Storm said. "You are not to be alone. Understood?" He glared at me.

I wanted to argue with him, to remind him I was an independent, mature adult.

Instead, I sighed. "I didn't want to be there by myself. It used to be a comfortable space. After what happened to Sadie, it gives me the creeps. If I wasn't alone, I might have been with Otis Skinner, and that could have been worse. Or Dominic King. We still can't be sure they weren't behind whoever came after me."

They might be waiting for an opportunity to deal

with me personally. That idea didn't reassure me. A laptop wouldn't be much use against a gun.

"No, we can't." Atlas leaned against the kitchen island, holding a bottle of water he hadn't opened since he pulled it out of the fridge half an hour ago. "I know the plan is to make them believe we're working with them, so we can bring them down from the inside. But I don't like Chelsea being anywhere near either of them. It might be better if you stop working for the team." He gave me an apologetic look, but the set of his jaw was determined. As unmoving as the expression on Storm's face.

"I second that," Frost said softly.

I frowned at him, but he shrugged. "I love you and I don't want anything to happen to you. If that means you take a break for a while, then..."

"I vote we leave it to Chelsea," Dallas said.

"Thank you," I told him. We all knew why he wanted me close, but it was nice to have a vote of confidence. Someone who recognised I was capable. Not just as a doctor, but my ability to keep an eye on Skinner and King.

"I vote she doesn't work there anymore," Storm said.

Jay looked from me to Atlas and back again,

clearly torn between supporting me and supporting him.

"Your votes don't matter," Ramsey said quietly, his skin slick with sweat, having come from the gym. Clearly he'd heard enough. "We need her there. You don't like it, take it up with Daze. Or Reuben Brantley. This goes above my head. Above all of yours, too. Including Chelsea."

I pressed my lips together and looked down at the floor for a few moments. If anything had the potential to make me want to walk away from the team, it was being told I was there as a pawn in the Brantley game. I knew I was, but being reminded was a nudge to my stubborn side to come out and play. Which, in this case, would do me no good whatsoever.

I looked back up. "That's settled then. I'll keep working for the team and do what I have to. Maybe I can help put an end to this sooner. We can get King and Skinner out, and away from the team, and get on with our lives."

Storm crossed his big arms over his chest, like he might have something to say that would stop me, regardless of Ramsey. "I don't fucking like it."

"Me either," Ramsey said. "We're in it now. Can't

stop it. Like Chelsea said, we can put an end to this sooner."

"Why don't we then?" Frost asked. "Can't we just kill King, Skinner and Coach Davis?"

"Not unless you want to deal with Carlos Jones and his cartel," Ramsey said. "We need to confirm it's him behind all of this. When we've done that, we can give the information to Brantley. Let him deal with Jones."

"We're just supposed to sit back and wait?" Storm grumbled. "Haven't we waited long enough?"

"No," Ramsey said simply. "It'll take what it takes. We don't want to provoke them."

"I want to provoke them," Storm said. "I want to provoke them so hard they can't walk for the rest of their lives. Which wouldn't be long after that anyway."

"Me too," Frost agreed. "What can I do to make this go faster? I'll pretend to be Dominic King's best friend if that helps."

"You're not going near him unless you have to," Storm told him. "Frost is right, though, what do we have to do?"

"I wish I knew." Ramsey wiped sweat off his forehead with a towel before draping it over his shoulder. "We still need to figure out who Nile Fox is."

"I have a feeling once we know, it'll answer a lot more other questions," Atlas said. He cracked open the lid of his water bottle and took a gulp. "How do we find that out?"

"I shouldn't have killed India," Dallas said quietly. "She might have had the answer."

"You did what you had to," I reminded him. "But that gives me an idea. India wasn't working alone. There must have been someone else. Someone at Flirts, or someone she lived with maybe?"

"You're not going back to work there," Storm growled.

"No, but I can go back socially," I said. "Or you can. Better if it's me, they think I'm harmless." Storm was many things, but harmless wasn't one of them.

"Not alone," Dallas said. "I'll go with you."

"Me too," Frost said.

"I'm in," Jay added.

"Any more than that and it will look suspicious," Ramsey said. "The rest of us will stay close."

Storm and Atlas both looked unimpressed, but for once, didn't argue. They knew Ramsey was right. If all of us turned up there, it wouldn't go unnoticed. Four of us would raise enough eyebrows as it was.

Should I try to insist a couple of them stay back?

Probably, but they wouldn't listen to me. Besides, I'd be safer with them around. I hoped.

"Tomorrow night," I said. "It'll be quieter on a Monday. I'll try to talk to Divina and see what she knows."

"Are we sure she's not in on it?" Frost asked. "She hired India. And Ivy, come to think of it."

"And Chelsea," Dallas pointed out. "If you're trying to suggest she hires shady people..."

"Some people would suggest I'm shady," I said.

Dallas moved over to wrap his arms around me. "You're not shady. If you were, you would have thrown that laptop without stopping to see who you were throwing it at. You wouldn't have cared as long as you were all right."

"I guess so," I said. "A doctor throwing computers around indiscriminately wouldn't be a good look, though. For the record, I'm glad I didn't throw anything at you."

"Me too." He kissed my forehead. "But, for the record, I would have caught it. I wouldn't be much of a footballer if I hadn't."

"Of course you would," I told him.

Frost chuckled. "I would have paid money to see that."

"How much?" Atlas asked. "For enough money, we could re-enact that here."

"No throwing computers in the house," Storm said. "If you're going to do it, do it outside where it won't make a mess. But really, don't do it," he added as Frost took a step towards the back door. "I don't want to be responsible for anyone getting a concussion from the corner of a PC."

Frost pointed a finger at him. "Right, that'd suck."

"Yep." Storm said. "Stick to throwing balls. Footballs," he added quickly, before anyone could take his words the wrong way.

"Thanks for clarifying," Atlas said. He tried to hold back a smile, but failed.

Storm flipped him off.

"You're right about this feeling like a houseful of brothers," I said to Dallas. "Who else would have conversations about throwing computers around like this?"

"I don't know," Dallas said. He scratched his forehead thoughtfully. "There might be other people out there as weird as us."

"If there is, I want to meet them," Frost said cheerfully. "They'd be awesome."

"No one is as weird as us," Jay said. "But we do it well."

"We do, don't we?" Frost offered him a fist bump.

Jay bumped his fist and offered him a slight smile.

Frost smiled back. They stayed locked there for a few moments before he leaned forward and kissed Jay's mouth.

"Weird, but pretty perfect," Frost whispered.

"Yeah, we are," Jay whispered back. "You wanna?"

"Yeah." Frost placed a hand on the back of Jay's head and leaned in to kiss him again.

Chapter Ten

Jay

Frost's mouth tasted like apples, sweet and fresh. They were his fruit of choice, along with bananas. Both kinds. Mine was currently standing at half-mast, but growing quickly.

Before I met Chelsea and him, I thought about sex as often as the average guy my age. Since meeting them, I seemed to be permanently hard. Or at least semi-hard. The best thing was, there was always someone around to help me with that. I'd lost count of how many orgasms I've had in the last couple of weeks. It wasn't too surprising that Dallas was addicted to Chelsea. I could get addicted to coming so often.

Frost's stubble scraped against mine, his tongue

pressing into my mouth. The guy definitely knew how to kiss. I was disappointed when he broke off.

"Do you want to go to your room where it's quieter?" he asked.

My heart thudded hard in my chest. "I love you," I said without thinking. "I love you and I love Atlas and I'd love Chelsea." I looked at each of them in turn. "You get me." They always understood what I needed, sometimes before I did.

"I love you too." Frost kissed the tip of my nose.

"So do I," Atlas said, sounding slowly choked, like he was trying to hold back emotions. For a big guy, who put on a mask of bravado, he felt things deeply. Being a part of this family meant as much to him as it did to me. Of course it did; why else would he put up with Storm?

"I love you too," Chelsea said. She put a hand on my bicep and softly kissed my mouth.

"Will you come with us?" I said to her and Atlas. "I'd like to be alone with the three of you."

"We'll be fine," Storm said. If he was put out, he didn't show it for once. Was he getting softer and more accepting as he got to know all of us? This might be the real him and he hadn't let anyone see it before. If that was the case, I hoped he showed that side of himself more often. I liked it.

Dallas didn't look so certain, but he stepped away to the kitchen.

Ramsey muttered something about having a shower before disappearing in the direction of his room.

"Let's go then." Frost laced his fingers in mine and tugged me behind him, in the direction of my bedroom.

The other guys had personalised their bedrooms with different furniture and art on the walls. In comparison, the room I shared with Atlas was simple and plain. The walls were bare and the furniture minimal. Bed, tables to either side, TV on a stand against the wall. Uncluttered and tidy, the way I liked it.

I felt all of that acutely as we stepped into the room. Like maybe Chelsea and Frost would take a look around and make suggestions for things I should change.

They didn't. Neither said a word as Chelsea closed the door behind her and everyone started to tear off their clothes. Socks, shirts and underwear went flying.

Atlas quickly shoved everything aside with his foot, making a pile which would have to be sorted through later. I could deal with that. I preferred my chaos to be organised. Since this resulted in three other naked people, I found I couldn't complain about the mess too much anyway. My attention was occupied taking in the view.

"Sometimes, I think I must be dreaming," I said slowly. "How did I get here, with all of you?"

"You must have won the lottery," Frost teased.

Atlas elbowed him. "We won the lottery when we found him."

"Huh, you're right," Frost said with a nod. "I won the lottery with all three of you."

"I'd say the same, but I don't buy lottery tickets," Chelsea said. "I've never been much of a gambler. Not like that."

Frost closed the distance between them. "What do you gamble with?"

She huffed out a brief laugh. "My life, apparently."

Atlas gripped her chin between his thumb and forefinger. "You know we'd never let anything happen to you, right? If anyone tries anything with any of you, I'll personally..." He shook his head.

"Tie them down and slice the skin off their body piece by piece?" Frost said helpfully.

Atlas pointed a finger gun at him with his spare hand. "Yes, that. For starters."

"You wouldn't do that to anyone," I told him.

Yes, I was well aware he killed people, but he didn't do shit like that for fun. Every time he took a life, it stole another piece of him. I'd tried a couple of times to get him to talk about it, but he refused, saying he didn't want to put the burden on me. I suspected he thought I'd turn away from him if he gave me too many details. He was wrong, I'd never turn away from him.

On the other hand, I was glad to be spared the details. I could imagine. That was enough.

"I would," Frost said. "In fact, I volunteer to save Atlas from the mess."

"That's all kinds of fucked up," Atlas told him.

Frost shrugged and grabbed my wrist to pull me towards the bed. "Yeah, and it's turning me on something fierce." That was obvious from his erection, bobbing as he walked.

"Frost wants a torture dungeon with sex room on the side," Chelsea said, following us over to the bed.

"Of course he does," I said. I wasn't even slightly surprised. When it came to our family, I was clean out of surprises. If they all told me they were secretly dragon shifters, I probably wouldn't blink. As long as they let me ride on their backs once in a while, I'd be here for it.

"I'm totally down for a sex room," Atlas said. He sat down beside us, his fist around his cock. "There has to be a sex swing. I've always wanted one of those. And one of those couch things."

"And what will you do with one of those couch things?" Chelsea asked. She rolled on to all floors and crawled over to him.

"I'd fuck you on it," he said. He grabbed her and turned her so her back was to him, her ass at the edge of the bed. He pried her legs apart and slid his fingers inside her. "I see you like the idea too, you're nice and wet." He put his fingers in and out of her a few times before sliding them out and replacing them with his cock.

"Frost," I said tentatively. "You want to... Do that to me?"

His eyes lit up. "Hell yeah I do. Have you got any — Ah." He reached over to the table beside the bed for the tube of lube we kept there.

I swallowed and turned my back on him. Atlas fucked my ass before, but no one else had. I usually kept that side of myself hidden from the world, sleeping with women instead. I couldn't remember when I realised I liked both; it was always a part of me. Acting on it, that took a long time, but it was worth the wait. This would be too.

The lube was cold as Frost pressed his fingers to my rear hole, smearing it around before sliding one of them inside me.

"Can I tell you something?" Frost said softly as he put the tube back on the table.

I looked over my shoulder at him. "Yeah, of course." My anxiety rose at the expression on his face, but it was tempered by Atlas and Chelsea's moans beside us.

"I've never done this to another guy before," he said, his eyes shifting back and forth like he was worried I'd judge him for it.

"I like that I'm your first," I said. That must have been the right thing to say, because he grinned and slid another finger inside me.

I shifted involuntarily with how good it felt. His hands were almost as big as Atlas', his fingers thick and broad.

He must have misread my shiver, because he drew them out a little. "Are you okay?"

"Better than okay," I assured him. "Don't stop. Please."

"Phew." He laughed softly and pushed them in deeper before adding a third finger.

I closed my eyes and focused on letting my muscles relax to take what he was giving me. I suspected it took me longer than it took other people, but after a minute or two I was ready for more.

"Fuck me," I whispered over my shoulder. "Please." I wrapped my hand around my cock and worked it up and down slowly as he positioned his and nudged into me.

"Happy to," he said, already sounding breathless. "You're so fucking tight, Jay. So fucking good." Bit by bit, he inched in until he was seated all the way inside me. He stopped then, letting me get used to him. Waiting for me to relax again.

I glanced over to where Atlas was thrusting into Chelsea with smooth, even strokes. His hands were on her breasts, pinching her nipples. Her eyes were closed as she rocked back onto him, keeping time with him.

His eyes were half closed, a smile on the corners of his lips. I loved to see him like that. Enjoying himself as he fucked our woman. I wished I had my phone with me so I could take a photo of the bliss on his face, and on hers. Instead, I committed the sight to memory, so I could picture it later and enjoy it again and again.

"You like what you see?" Frost whispered. "I know I do. One of the best things about being part of this family is being able to watch that. And do it." He slid halfway out of me before pushing back in. "You feel so good."

"So do you," I said. The way he filled me, it felt different from Atlas somehow, but just as good. He was slightly longer and hit me at a different angle, that must be it. Atlas' cock was a little thicker. Both of them were perfect.

His hands gripping my hips, he started to thrust in and out slowly and carefully, gradually increasing the speed as I pumped myself faster.

"I'm going to come," Chelsea cried out.

"Come for us," Atlas told her. He thrust into her faster too, pulling out all the way before slamming back in. His face was strained like he was also on the verge of orgasm.

I'd seen that look so many times, but I'd never get enough of it. Never get enough of him, or Frost or Chelsea. They were everything to me. I wasn't sure what I could do to keep them safe, but I'd sure as hell try.

In the meantime, I rocked back into Frost, driving him harder as Chelsea came, quickly followed by Atlas.

Frost groaned, long and low before he also came, spilling himself into me. "Bloody hell, so fucking good..." He pumped a couple of more times before finally sliding out of me.

Before I knew what he was doing, he'd rolled me onto my back and wrapped his mouth around my cock. It only took a couple of sucks before I lost myself, coming hard and fast down his throat.

He grinned over at me, slid his lips off me and crawled up so his face was in front of mine. He arched his eyebrow questioningly. When I nodded, he pressed his mouth to mine, squirting my own cum between my lips.

"That's fucking hot," Atlas whispered.

Chelsea murmured her agreement, locking her eyes on mine as I swallowed.

"You guys are everything," she said. "Everything and then some."

As I licked my lips all I could do was nod my agreement.

Chapter Eleven

Chelsea

"Sweetheart, you can't stay away, can you?" Divina bustled over to hug me. "Are you sure you don't want to come back and work for me?"

Music pumped through the club, loud and provocative, but I didn't know the curvaceous girl who danced on the stage today. Judging by a hint of awkwardness in her moves here and there, she was new. The way she peeled off her bra and dropped it aside spoke of her self-consciousness.

I was reminded of the first time I was up there, certain customers would walk away after taking one look at me. Of course, they hadn't. They hadn't been able to tear their eyes away as I slowly peeled off the layers I was wearing, revealing more and more of me. If I was a little slow, no one seemed to give a shit.

The men avidly crowded around the stage now didn't care either. They'd come to watch a gorgeous woman dance. That was all they saw. They loved every move of her curvy body, skilled or not.

I squeezed Divina and kissed her cheek before stepping back. "I'm absolutely sure. I miss you, but that part of my life is in my past. Sorry." In a not-sorry kind of way.

She pouted playfully. "I don't think you are sorry, but I'll forgive you. What can I do for you? You and those men of yours here look intense." She didn't seem concerned. If anything, she was curious, regarding each of them in turn. There wasn't much she hadn't seen in her years owning Flirts.

I wondered what it'd take to really surprise her. The only time I remembered seeing anything close to that from her, was when we found India. Even then, she didn't seem shocked. Sad and worried, but not surprised. I wished I could be as strong as she was. As hard to rattle.

"Can we talk in your office?" I jerked my head towards it.

"It must be serious." She gestured for us to walk ahead of her. Dallas, Frost and I did, while Jay lingered behind.

Storm, Atlas and Ramsey were gathered outside, keeping an eye on things there.

"It is," I said.

She stepped inside, turned and sat on the edge of her desk.

I stood in the middle of the room, Frost on one side of me, Dallas on the other.

Jay stayed in the doorway, standing sideways so he could keep an eye on us and the rest of the club.

"Out with it then." Divina gestured with her fingers. "What's so important you'd come all the way down here with a contingent of bodyguards?"

"We aren't bodyguards," Dallas mumbled.

Frost, on the other hand, looked pleased to be referred to that way. Jay seemed indifferent.

"I was wondering if India was close with anyone, as far as you knew?" I saw no reason to beat around the proverbial bush. Divina was a busy woman and wouldn't want us to waste her time.

"Someone suspicious," Frost added.

Divina raised a shapely eyebrow at him. "I thought that was what you meant." She smirked slightly, but he grinned and shrugged. Typical Frost.

She hummed and slid her gaze from him, back at me. "You know what she was like. She was friends with everyone. Everyone loved her. I don't think there's a person here who wouldn't have called her friend."

It was my turn to hum in response. She was right about that. We all adored her and, as far as I could remember, India gave everyone an equal amount of her time.

Divina would have seen a lot more than I did though. She practically lived here.

"Anyone in particular though?" I pressed. "Someone she was tight with? Someone working security? A customer even?"

Divina toyed with a huge ring on her finger. Silver with some kind of purple stone. I'd never seen her without it.

"If I had to suggest she was particularly close to anyone, I'd say Tina and Sierra. Tina left right after you did, but Sierra is still here. She's been guarded since India was killed. I mean, keeping her thoughts to herself, not literally guarded." She eyed the guys again. "But we've all been on edge."

In the corner of my eye, I saw Dallas look down toward the floor.

Quickly, I said, "I can't blame you. When things like that happen it's... Scary." I glanced around the space as subtly as I could.

Divina probably had more weapons in her office

than the laptop that sat on the desk. I wouldn't be surprised if there was a gun in the top drawer, or a knife or two. She wouldn't hesitate to use them if she had to. Divina was as tough as they came. She had to be. If anyone around here was a badass, it was her.

She also had the biggest heart of anyone I ever met. The staff loved her for a reason. She took care of everyone like they were family. She was like a second mother to me. Or a wise aunt. If I could be half the woman when I was her age, I'd be doing very well for myself.

"Yeah, they are scary, and if Sierra is involved, she can hit the road," Divina said unapologetically. "I don't want any more of that shit here. The girls that work for me, I want to keep them safe. They shouldn't have to look over their shoulders all night, wondering if they'll be next. If Sierra is into some shit, or going to cause any trouble, she can get the hell out."

"Do you mind if I talk to her?" I asked. "She might not be involved in anything, but if we can get to the bottom of it, it'll put your mind at ease."

"I'm not sure I'd go that far, but you can try," Divina said. "Do me a favour and don't make a mess."

Frost was quick to say, "We won't."

Dallas slid him a look, but he didn't say anything.

Frost shrugged. "We really won't."

"You can find her in the changing area," Divina said. "Go and do whatever you have to do." She waved us away and stepped around her desk to sink into the chair. "I'll be busy here for a while."

In other words, whatever we did, she didn't know anything about it. She wouldn't take responsibility for it. She wasn't happy, but she wouldn't interfere either.

"Let's go," I said to the guys. "Thank you, Divina."

She opened her laptop and turned it on, giving me a small glance and nod before returning her attention to the screen.

As we stepped away, Jay said, "Are you sure she's not involved?"

"No," I admitted after a few moments thought. "I have to trust that she's not."

I didn't want to think she was working against us. People like her, they did whatever they had to do to cover their asses. She'd look out for her own interests before she looked out for ours.

I didn't blame her. I'd do the same thing. I *was* doing the same thing. Confronting one of her employees could ultimately be bad for her business, but we had no choice. The fact she was letting us do it suggested to me she wasn't working against us. She wanted to stay the hell out of any trouble, that was all.

I hoped I was reading the situation right. Otherwise, we could be fucked.

"Are you okay?" I slipped my hand into Dallas' and glanced over into his troubled face. "Being back here can't be easy."

The first time we met here in Flirts was intense. He'd been disgusted at himself for being with me and stormed out of the room. Things certainly had changed since then.

Of course, the last time he was here, he took a life. This place must hold conflicting memories for him. Difficult ones.

"Kind of." He had to raise his voice to be heard over the music as we stepped closer to the door that led into the change area. "I'll be okay." His stoic, football player mask was firmly in place. "Let's just do this."

I squeezed his hand, then turned my attention to Gary, the security guard who stood beside the door. "Hey, Gaz."

"Hey, Chels!" The gentle giant leaned down to give me a hug. "You coming back to work here? We've missed you."

"I missed you too." I squeezed him quickly before

letting him go, not wanting the guys to get the wrong idea.

Gary and I were friends from the first day I started at Flirts. No one looked after the girls better than he did. If anyone tried anything, he'd escort them out the door, whether they liked it or not. I never saw him hit anyone, but they didn't get away with any shit while he was around either. Honestly, most of them took one look at him and backed right off.

"I'm not coming back to work, I just came to have a quick chat with Sierra. Divina said she was out back?" I smiled sweetly, hoping he wouldn't become suspicious. If he thought we were up to something, he wouldn't hesitate to escort us out too regardless of what Divina said. He wanted trouble even less than she did.

"Last time I saw her, she was," he agreed. "Go on in. It might make you nostalgic enough to change your mind and come back." He winked.

"You never know," I said with a laugh. I couldn't help but appreciate the way he and Divina made me feel welcome here. They always had. We were a little family, even after I left.

He pulled out a key, unlocked the door and held it open for us to step past. All the while keeping an eye on the crowd in case anyone thought to slip in too.

I exchanged glances with the guys once Gary closed the door behind us. Being back here should have felt familiar, even comforting, but the click of the door made the hairs on the back of my neck stand up. The same feeling of unease I felt in the infirmary came crashing back.

"We're right here," Frost said. "I've sent the others a text to tell them where we are. Nothing is going to happen to us." He tucked his phone into the pocket of his track pants and patted it.

"Yeah I...hope so," I said. There were more dangerous places in Dusk Bay than the back of a strip club, but the unease lingered. "Let's get this over with."

Still holding onto Dallas' hand, I led the way down to the dressing rooms. "She should be in here." I stopped in the doorway, mindful that there might be naked people inside, who wouldn't appreciate the intrusion.

Only a couple of women sat applying make-up, both fully dressed. Milly sat to the left, Sierra to the right. Blonde hair in a stark contrast to dark. One slender, the other curvy. Divina offered variety, so there was a dancer for every eye.

"Hey," I greeted them both cheerfully. "Sierra, have you got a minute, honey?" I wanted to appear as non-threatening as possible. I didn't want her to run or clamp up.

She looked up at my reflection in the mirror. "Chels! It's so good to see you again. Of course I have a minute for you, darling." She rose and took in the three large men behind me. Her eyebrows were the next thing to rise. "Well this is interesting," she said lightly. "Is everything okay?"

"Maybe we should talk out in the corridor," I suggested, giving Milly half an eye.

"I was just leaving," Milly said. She shot up out of her chair and hurried out of the room, barely glancing back.

We had to step out of her way to let her pass. I caught a whiff of rose-scented perfume, similar to the one I wore when I worked here. It was mixed with the smell of soap and hairspray. All familiar. If I was inclined to be nostalgic, that would do it.

"She's new," Sierra said. "Still trying to get her head around working in a place like this." She'd seen the same thing a dozen times before, as I had. Even women who loved the work had an adjustment period at the beginning. Taking your clothes off for money took some getting used to.

The first time I did it, I was terrified. Certain there'd be no audience for all the imperfections I perceived myself to have. I quickly learned I was the only one who cared about them. If anything, the guys who came to watch me, embraced them. They liked that I wasn't perfect, because they weren't either. They came to see a confident woman, and pretend she was dancing for them.

"I'm sure she'll be fine." I gave Sierra a quick hug. "How have you been?"

"Fine, but I don't think you came to ask me how I am," she said. "Is this anything to do with India and what happened to her?"

Her words were immediately followed by the deafening crack of a gunshot.

Chapter Twelve

Chelsea

Strong arms grabbed me and I was pulled to the ground, surrounded by a protective wall of muscle. I ducked my head and screwed my eyes shut, as though somehow that would protect me from a bullet.

For the longest time, we crouched like that, hard up against the wall. My heart was in my throat the entire time, thundering like crazy.

In the back of my mind was the unwelcome thought, *Fuck, not again.*

Finally, I managed to say, "Is everyone okay?"

Slowly, I opened my eyes and looked into Jay's. He was opposite me, with Frost and Dallas on either side. His brown eyes were wide, staring at me without blinking.

"I'm okay," he whispered.

"Me too," Frost agreed. "Dallas?"

"Fine," Dallas said. "What... What happened?"

It wasn't until he spoke that I realised the tang of blood filled my nostrils. If all of us were okay, then...

Biting my lip, I turned to look at where Sierra stood. Now, she lay on the ground, blood seeping from a hole in her chest, directly above her heart.

"Fuck," I whispered. My instinct was to try to help her, but she was beyond help. I swivelled my gaze to the door. "I didn't see anyone."

"Me either," Frost said. "My eyes were on her." Slowly, he released his grip on us and stood.

"I saw," Jay said, slowly rising as well. "It was that other girl, Milly. I saw the gun in her hand and pulled all of you down."

I realised now, he was right. He started to push us to the ground before the gunshot sounded. If he hadn't...

"My hero." Frost kissed his mouth. "We need to find her." He headed towards the door.

Dallas was the last to stand, trembling, his eyes on Sierra. "It happened again." His tone was haunted. For the rest of my life, I'd remember the look in his eyes.

I grabbed his arm. "It wasn't you. You didn't do this."

He couldn't seem to stop staring at her. "I came here again and someone died. What if... What if it was you?" He shook his head.

I placed my hands on his shoulders and turned him to face me. "It wasn't me. You didn't do this. This is not your fault. I don't know why Milly did it, but it wasn't because of anything you did. Okay?"

I wished I believed that. Milly was either aiming at one of us, or was trying to stop Sierra from talking to us. Either way, this was my fault. I was the one who decided to come here. If I hadn't, Sierra would still be alive.

For how long though? I didn't know, but a while at least.

"We should go before she comes back," Jay said. His phone was in his hand, presumably filling Atlas in on what happened.

"Looking for someone?" Storm asked as he stepped into the doorway, a small body over his shoulder. Milly writhed and struggled, but his arm was clamped over her, holding her firmly in place.

"She came running out with a gun in her hand, so we figured we should grab her," Atlas said. He glanced around us to Sierra, his expression grim. "Looks like we were right. Is everyone okay?"

"We're fine," I said. "Everyone except for her."

Divina wasn't going to be happy. Technically, we didn't make a mess, but another woman was dead. And two girls would be missing from tonight's lineup.

If she wanted to, she could take it out on Milly when we were done with her.

"Looks like we're going to have a chat with this woman then," Storm said. "Unless she wants to give us some answers now." He glanced back over his shoulder.

"Let me go," Milly insisted. "You have the wrong person." She wriggled harder, but it got her nowhere. He was approximately twice her size and at least twice as strong. Not to mention angry. That alone would keep her pinned there until he was ready to let her go.

"Gun says otherwise." Ramsey appeared, carrying a small handgun. "Recently fired." He held it between his thumb and forefinger, a look of disgust in his eyes. Not for the gun, but for what it was used for. The gun itself was just a tool, albeit a deadly one. Milly was the one at fault here.

"Definitely by her," Jay said. "I saw her do it." He explained in a handful of words.

"Care to rethink your answer?" Storm asked. He looked ready to snap her neck and throw her in the bay.

"Fuck off." She tried to kick him in the back, but he turned, almost hitting her head against the door frame. She managed to duck her head to the side at the last moment. "Hey, watch it!"

He turned back around the other way, almost doing the same thing, and not looking even slightly sorry for it. If anything, he seemed to be enjoying himself. Of course he was. She was lucky he hadn't strangled her the moment he realised what she did. Or what she might have done if they hadn't caught up with her first. "We can take her to your brother's workroom," Storm said.

Her head picked up and she looked at me, terror in her eyes.

Yeah, she knew exactly who I was and who my brother was. And what he was going to do to her. Why hadn't that stopped her from raising a gun in my presence?

If I was as scared as she seemed to be now, I wouldn't have done it. No matter how much I got paid.

Was it that simple though? Probably not. It usually wasn't. She could have a family member being held somewhere to ensure her obedience. A sibling or maybe a child. If not that, they might have something on her that forced her to act.

People who hired other people to kill for them, there was nothing they wouldn't do to get what they wanted. No low they wouldn't reach if they felt they had to. They wouldn't lose any sleep over it either. This was exactly why I tried to stay away from this lifestyle. I didn't want to become a monster like that. Cold and unfeeling. Numb.

"It's not too late to speak," I told her. If she really was forced to do this, we might go easier on her.

She dropped her head and sagged against Storm's shoulder.

"Seems she'd rather deal with your brother than with whoever put her up to shooting Sierra," Atlas mused. "I'm guessing she knows she's dead either way."

"Not necessarily," I said, knowing she was listening. "She might open up later and be allowed to get back to her life. You know my brother doesn't kill innocent people. She could have been paid to try to scare us and things got out of hand."

Her head picked up again. "That's exactly what

happened. I've never used a gun before. I didn't know how to. I thought it wasn't loaded, or it was locked or something. Hell, it could have been a toy for all I knew. I didn't know anyone would die."

"Of course you didn't," I said, although I didn't believe a word that came out of her mouth. "I know you didn't mean to kill Sierra. It was a terrible accident."

Milly nodded vigourously. "Exactly. So, if this big oaf would put me down, I can get out of here. Before someone else tries to pin this on me." Her voice rose higher and higher as she spoke. She was trying to look like she wasn't going to lose it, but she was starting to freak out around the edges. I would be too if I was her.

"I don't think so." I frowned. "No doubt my brother will have questions for you. He'd be very disappointed if I didn't give him a chance to get answers."

I wasn't saying that to scare her. He *would* want to see her. There was a chance he'd know who she was and who she was working for, even if Ramsey didn't.

Not to mention the trouble we'd be in if we let her go and she proved to be someone important or useful. That was a call I wasn't willing to make. And

Ramsey didn't seem inclined to make it either. He was as quiet as ever, turning the gun around and around in his hands, his eyes on it like he was trying to figure something out. What, I had no idea. Whatever it was, he was deep in thought about it.

The fact he didn't use the gun on Milly was something to be grateful for. I'd seen enough bloodshed for one night. For now at least.

Milly dropped her head again and sighed. She'd probably stick to the story I'd given her, but she knew we weren't going to let her go that easily.

I *almost* felt sorry for her. If I thought she really was innocent, I would have. But I didn't. She was in this up to her eyeballs. I suspected it was her who was working with India, not Sierra. By suspecting the wrong person, I might have caused an innocent woman to lose her life. For that, I'd always feel like shit.

I took a long look back at Sierra before following the guys out. "I'm sorry," I told her corpse.

I sent a message off to my brother to let him know we were coming and to request someone come and clean in here. It was the least I could do for Sienna and Divina. I wished I could do more, but I needed to be there to talk to Milly. I wanted to hear what she had to say, Besides, sometimes a woman was needed to make another woman open up. I desperately needed to understand why she did what she did.

Was she really aiming at me? If she was, I owed Jay my life. If he hadn't seen her when he had, things would have turned out very different.

"Chelsea?" Dallas slipped an arm around me and held me close to his body. He was still trembling, but it lessened a fraction.

"I'm coming," I said. "I feel so bad for Sierra. She couldn't have gotten out of the way of the bullet in time. She probably didn't even see the gun. One minute she was talking to us, and the next minute..." A knot of emotion filled my throat. My eyes prickled with tears.

"When I heard the gunshot, I thought it hit you," he whispered. "I thought another one might come. All I could do was hold you and try to put myself between it and you. I don't care if I could have died as long as you didn't."

"I would have been devastated if you died." I leaned against him and buried my face in his shoulder. "If any of you died."

I was starting to think we should go home and stay there forever. We could have food and whatever else we needed delivered and never have to see anyone but each other, right? We might go crazy, but at least we'd be alive.

"I don't hate that idea," he admitted. "We could stay in bed all day."

"We need to get out of here first," Atlas said from behind us. "We can work out a plan later. For the record, I think people would notice if we didn't turn up to training or to games. Sooner or later, they'd come looking for us. 'They' being the press and team management."

I grimaced. The last thing we needed was a contingent of paparazzi camped outside our gates, wondering what the hell we were up to.

"Fine, we'll be normal for a while longer." I untangled myself from Dallas, but kept my arms around him, walking with him to the corridor and down to the door that led out of the club.

"Who said anything about normal?" Atlas said lightly. "I just said we can't hide away, that's all."

"Watch your mouth," Frost told him. "Normal is a dirty word, don't you know?"

Atlas clapped him on the shoulder. "Sorry, bro. I'll watch myself from now on."

For now, we watched ourselves, stepping out carefully to join the others.

Storm tossed Milly into the back of his SUV,

where she landed with a bounce and short cry of protest.

"Sorry not sorry," he said before he closed the hatch to lock her in.

She looked suitably miserable. She should thank her lucky stars she wasn't dead.

Yet.

We all squeezed into the rest of the vehicle and fell silent as we made our way to Ice's place.

Chapter Thirteen

Chelsea

THE DOOR TO THE WORKROOM WAS SLIGHTLY ajar when we arrived. Storm, once again, carried Milly over his shoulder. She'd tried to leap out of the back of the SUV when he opened it, but he grabbed her before her feet hit the ground.

If he hadn't, the others were arrayed around behind him, ready for her to try exactly that. He tossed her like a sack of potatoes and marched with her sulking, but firmly held in place.

When Ramsey pushed open the door and led us inside, my brother wasn't alone.

He stood beside his worktable, a chair pulled up to it. A man sat in the chair, one arm chained above his head. His opposite hand was on a laptop keyboard. He looked exhausted and scared.

I wrinkled my nose at the tang of blood.

"Whose choice is it?" Ice asked, his tone sweetly venomous. He leaned over the man, looking him right in the face.

The man whispered something.

"Say it again," Ice insisted. "We have visitors and they didn't hear." He gripped the top of the man's head and turned his face towards us.

"Women's," the man said in a whimper. "It's women's choice. Everything, always. It's their bodies."

"Exactly." Ice patted him on the head like he was a dog. "Be a good boy and tell your followers what you tried to do."

With his one free hand, the man frantically tapped at his keyboard.

Ice turned to us and grinned. "Sometimes I indulge in side projects. Only ones that are deserved."

I had some idea who the man was, and he got no sympathy from me.

"That's what happens when you fuck around," Frost said. "Sometimes, you find out."

"Precisely." Ice nodded. "Now, you have someone for me?"

"Do you have to look so happy about it?" I asked.

"Firstly, yes." He counted it off on one finger. "And secondly, yes. I was getting bored with this asshole, and I'm always happy to see all of you. Who do we have here?" He stepped around Storm, bent over and peered up at Milly.

"Millicent Nelson-Thorne, what have I said about ending up here?" He clicked his tongue.

"It wasn't my idea," she said. "Blame these id— People." She had enough sense not to refer to us as idiots in front of my brother. "I was minding my own business. Can I go now?"

"No," Storm snapped. "You aimed a gun at my woman. You're lucky I haven't snapped your scrawny neck."

She tried to kick his stomach. "My neck is not scrawny. At least I have a neck."

Ice straightened, his expression turning dark. "Care to explain yourself? You should know better than to aim anything at my sister. Except compliments. Those are always acceptable."

"They happened to be there," she said with a sigh. "It was Sierra they wanted. I made sure they saw me and got out of the way."

I glanced at Jay, who shrugged.

"It might be true," he said. "It all happened so fast."

She lifted her head and glared at him. "Of course it's true. I'm not a liar."

I snorted. "Just a killer."

"A girl has to eat," she protested. "Can I go now?"

"Who hired you?" Ice asked. "Why did they want you to kill her?"

"I didn't stick around to ask questions," she insisted. "You know how it works. They wanted it taken care of and I did it. Do you think I wanted to kill her? She was one of the nice ones." She flopped her head back down against Storm's shoulder.

"Who's they?" Frost asked.

"Unless you'd like to enjoy an extended stay here, I'd find the answer to the question," Ice suggested. "Like I said, I was getting bored with this prick." He jerked his thumb at the man who was still frantically typing.

"I don't know, but she was tight with India," Milly said. "And India was tight with that Dominic King guy. He'd been... You know, visiting her, if you get what I mean."

"Fucking her," I said. "It might have been him who wanted Sierra killed. To keep her from telling anyone what India told her."

"I'm not naming names because I don't want to end up dead, but yes," Milly said. She let out a long, defeated sigh. "You might as well kill me. If he knows I'm here, I'm dead already."

"Do you often kill people for Dominic King?" Frost asked.

"Or anyone else?" Dallas added.

"I work for whoever hires me," she said. "I had a bad feeling about this one from the start. I should have listened to my instincts."

"She's mostly harmless," Ice said. "Just a pawn for the higher ups. King wouldn't care if we cut her throat and threw her into the bay. Neither would Reuben Brantley, or Daze."

"Exactly, I'm nobody," Milly said. She looked back up again, a ray of hope in her eyes. "You could help me disappear. I don't mean kill me; just, I don't know, let me take off out of Dusk Bay. I promise I'll get the hell out and stay out of your way. Or I could work for you. I'm good at doing all sorts of shit."

She looked around at all of us. "I didn't mean it when I said you don't have a neck." She twisted around to look back at Storm. "You totally have a neck. Actually, you kinda smell good." She took a long sniff.

He jerked his shoulder back and forth. "Stop that. You don't get to smell me."

"Not my fault," she said. "You're the one holding

me over your shoulder. I have nowhere to go but here. If you put me down, I'll go wherever you want me to go. You never have to see me again if you don't want to."

I glanced over to Ramsey and Ice. I found it hard not to like her, but letting her go wasn't my call to make. It seemed to me like she got in over her head and now all she wanted to do was get out of it. I could relate to that.

"I suppose we can let you go," Ice conceded finally.

"Yes." She fist pumped the air. "I'll stay out of your way, promise."

"And you won't take any jobs to kill anyone in this room," Ramsey added. "Otherwise you're as good as dead."

"Noted," she said. "No killing any of you. Not even that asshole?" She glanced over to the man who stopped typing to stare at us. He started again when he realised we were looking.

"He's all mine," Ice said. "Storm, you can put her down."

"Wait," I said quickly. When everyone's eyes turned to me, I turned mine on Milly. "Do you know who Nile Fox is?"

She stared at me for a moment before she burst

into giggles. "Do you mean Nyla Fox? She's one of the Crimson Vipers. She sticks to the shadows, but rumour has it she's trying to position herself to be Carlos Jones' successor. She's a nasty piece of work. If I were you, I'd stay away from her."

"How do you know who she is?" I asked.

"I listen to gossip," she said. "You know people tell us things they wouldn't say to anyone else. Some of the cartel guys frequent Flirts. I'm a favourite of some of them." She shrugged modestly. "But you didn't hear any of this from me. Be careful, they say she's more ruthless than Carlos Jones. He's a pussycat in comparison to her. Now, can you put me down?"

Gradually, Storm lowered her to the ground. The moment her feet touched, she bolted for the door.

"Are you sure that's a good idea?" Frost asked Ice.

"She really is harmless." Ice turned back to his other guest. "Unlike this prick. He tried to get too handsy with a woman without her consent. You know how I feel about men like that. Shame you weren't here an hour ago, you would have been able to watch me redecorate him so he'll never try anything with another woman again." He smiled.

"He's lucky I'm not the sort of person to give him what he tried to give her. A guy has to have limits."

"It's not worth stooping to his level," I agreed. "Hopefully whatever he's writing will reach other people like him."

"Hopefully," Ice agreed. "Otherwise I'm going to need a bigger workroom."

"That reminds me," Frost said, looking excited. "I wanted to talk to you about a workroom of our own."

While the pair chatted about torture devices, I stepped over to Dallas, who'd retreated to the corner of the room.

"I could have sworn she said Nile," he said when I got close enough to hear him whisper. "If I got it right in the first place..."

"We still wouldn't have known," I said. "I've never heard of her. If she's as bad as Milly said, then I don't want to meet her. Milly might have the right idea about getting out of Dusk Bay." We couldn't leave, we both knew that, but it was tempting.

"You think she's who is behind all of this?" Dallas asked. "She might be the one trying to muscle in on the Brantley's territory."

I thought about that for a minute or two.

"I suspect it's more than that," I said finally. "She

might be trying to replace them, and Carlos. If she managed that, she'd be incredibly powerful."

She might not stop at Dusk Bay. That much power would become addictive and she'd want more and more of it. People like that, they didn't care who they stepped on in their quest for power. Whether it was us, or half the city, she wouldn't flinch. Whatever it took to win.

"What do we do?" he asked. His brow was corrugated with a deep frown, eyes more troubled than I'd seen them yet. Blaming himself for mishearing, even though it really wouldn't have made a difference in the long run.

But it mattered to him, so it mattered to me. If it was allowed to fester, like an untreated wound, it would eat him up inside.

I shook my head. "I have no idea."

I had a bad feeling about this from the start. Now, it at least doubled. Possibly tripled.

I felt like we were living that scene in the first *Star Wars* movie, where the walls of the garbage compactor were pressing in on the characters. Threatening to squash them into nothing. All that was missing was the literal dirty water. And a handy android to turn the compactor off from the outside.

"I won't let anything happen to you," he said quickly. He wrapped his arms around me and held me close, like the embrace would keep me safe from the world.

"I know you won't," I said. "I won't let anything happen to you either." Maybe it was time to practice my gun and knife skills. They were rusty to say the least. Put either weapon in my hand and it would probably come back to me like riding a bike. What choice did I have? If anyone came for us, I needed to be prepared.

"Ice loves the idea of our own workroom," Frost said, coming up beside us. "He's going to help us put it together." He was bouncing on the balls of his feet and like he was ready to jump up and down. His smile was like a little boy allowed to go into a toy shop and choose anything he wanted. Or one who found everything he ever dreamt of, sitting under the tree on Christmas morning. When he'd embraced the darker side of himself, he did it with enthusiasm. For him, there was no looking back.

"That's great," I said absently.

Who needed literal dirty water when the figurative kind dragged you under against your will? For so many years, I'd fought against the current, only to have it engulf all of us like a tsunami. The battle I'd fought for so long, was it one I'd never win? Right then, it felt like it.

Whether I wanted to or not, I was a part of the darker side of Dusk Bay. I had two choices: sink or swim.

Chapter Fourteen

Chelsea

The moment we got back to the mansion, the guys all exchanged looks and disappeared in opposite directions without a word. All except Dallas, who took my hand and led me to my room. All of the room had ensuite bathrooms, with big baths, but mine was the biggest.

That's where he took me, keeping his fingers laced in mine while turning the water on.

"I can do that myself," I protested.

"I know, but I want to do it for you," he said. "It's been a long day. And night."

He was right about that. It was almost midnight.

I was tired, but too wired to sleep right now anyway. My mind was buzzing like crazy, thoughts tumbling over and over in my mind like a clothes dryer. Turning in an endless circle without any answers. It seemed like the more we knew, the more we needed to know.

Did I want to know more? Not really, but I had to. Like it or not, we were in this up to our eyeballs. Where it would end I had no idea, but we had to see it through. If we didn't, it would force us to anyway. If we ran from Dusk Bay, it wouldn't be far enough, no matter where we ended up. Trouble would always be a step behind.

Or ahead.

"It's a lot," I said softly.

He took a bath bomb from the shelf, opened it and dropped it into the water. "Yeah, it is." He squeezed my hand and we stood together, watching the water rise, the steam like misty fingers climbing towards the ceiling.

That was all we did for several minutes, until the water was high enough. He reached over to turn off the tap and face me. He offered me the faintest smile before starting to help me out of my clothes.

I could do that too, but I decided not to argue. If this would help him to get his head around everything, then who was I to argue? Besides, it was nice to be spoilt once in a while. A girl could get used to it.

Once I was naked, my clothes in a pile on the floor, he took my hand again and helped me to step into the water. I lowered myself down and closed my eyes.

"This is perfect." I exhaled softly.

"You're perfect," he told me. He scooped up my clothes and put them aside before stripping off his own. He climbed into the bath behind me, his legs to either side, and wrapped his arms around me. His cock nudged my ass, but all he did for now was hold me.

I leaned back against him and let the water slowly wash away the stress and anxiety.

"This is cosy," Atlas remarked.

I opened my eyes and looked over to where he stood, a glass of wine in his hand. He smiled and handed it to me before disappearing out of the bathroom. A few moments later, Storm entered, a plate in his hand.

"Where did you get chocolate covered strawberries from?" I asked while gratefully taking the plate and inhaling the sweet smell.

"I have my ways." His gaze lingered on my bare body before he too slipped out of the bathroom.

"Did you guys organise this without me realising?" I asked.

"Nope," Dallas said. "I think we all knew what you needed."

"And you call me perfect," I said. I took a sip of wine before setting it down on the side of the bath. I was about to try a strawberry when Dallas took the plate from my hand.

"Let me do that." He picked one up and pressed it against my lips.

I opened my mouth and took a bite. "Mmm, that's so good." The perfect combination of sweet and a hint of acidity.

His cock hardened a little at my moan.

"This is good." He bit into a strawberry of his own. "Maybe we can stay like this for a few hours and let the others wait on us."

"That's a good idea because you forgot something important." Frost entered the bathroom, carrying an arm full of candles. He placed them around the room before lighting them one by one and then turning off the light. "That's much better."

"My bad," Dallas said. He didn't seem too concerned. "Thanks, bro."

"Any time, bro." Frost leaned over to kiss me before stepping back out of the bathroom.

I peered at the door. "It's not like we don't have everything we need, but I'm wondering if Jay and Ramsay are up to anything."

"I was wondering the same thing," Dallas said. "Maybe they're bringing you the heads of your enemies. That might take some time."

"Especially given we don't know exactly who our enemies are," I agreed.

Honestly, I didn't want a disembodied head, but if it meant this was all over, then maybe it wouldn't be so bad. Just this once. I would prefer they not make a habit of it.

Jay stepped into the doorway and tapped on the frame. "Hey, would it be too corny if I played you something on my guitar?" He held up his hand, his fingers curled around the neck of his instrument.

"I didn't know you played, but that would be perfect," I said. I should have guessed that was coming next. If not an actual instrument, then speakers and soothing music.

"I'm not the best guitarist in the world." He shrugged, leaned against the vanity, positioned the guitar and started to play the opening chords of *Hallelujah*. That was followed by a ballad from Wolf Venom, and then one by Ice Blue Roses.

"You're putting me to shame," Ramsey remarked. He'd stepped into the bathroom halfway through the second song. He also carried a guitar.

"I can't help being awesome," Jay said, humble in spite of the words. "Do you know this one?" He played a few chords before raising an eyebrow at Ramsey.

"Course I do." Ramsey leaned against the wall and played the next few chords of what I recognised as an Abbie Hart song.

Jay joined in again and the pair played together, Ramsey singing softly and in key.

"I've never been serenaded before," I said to Dallas.

His body rumbled as he chuckled. "Me either. Especially not while in the bath with a beautiful woman. I think I'll stay here forever."

"Me too." I sipped wine while leaning against him and watching the other guys play.

This was like something out of a dream, or a movie. The whole world melted away and all that was left was us and this moment. Six wonderful guys all working together to make me feel special. Somehow, they all knew what I needed in order to unwind and forget about things for a while.

I couldn't help myself; I fell in love with each of them a little more. Chances were, I'd never fully understand why or how I got so lucky, but I was counting every single blessing. If I could capture this moment in a bottle, I'd keep it close forever. As it was, I savoured it, committing it all to memory, in case everything came crashing down around us tomorrow.

In unison, Jay and Ramsey finished the song and bowed over their guitars.

Careful not to spill my wine in the bath, I clapped. "That was so good. When you finish playing football, maybe you should join a band."

"I've always wanted to be a rock star," Ramsey said wistfully. "But only if you'll go on tour with me. Otherwise, I'll keep my music for times like this."

"What he said," Jay agreed. "It's fun once in a while, but I don't think I want to do it all day. I'll play for you anytime you want me to, though."

"Me too," Ramsey said. To Jay he added, "Any time you want to jam, hit me up. I'm always down for a session."

"I'd like that," Jay said, suddenly looking shy and awkward. "I haven't had anyone to play with for a long time. It's... Kinda... My happy place, you know?"

Ramsey grinned. "Mine too. One of them, anyway. After football and the gym." He lowered his guitar. "I might put this away, the steam isn't good for it."

"Yeah, good idea." Jay followed him out the door, leaving us in silence and the light of a dozen flickering candles.

Chapter Fifteen

Chelsea

I woke like I often did these days, with Dallas parting my legs and sliding his cock into me. He let out a long breath, his eyes closed against the morning light that peeked through the curtains.

"What would I do without you?" he whispered.

"What would any of us do?" Frost asked from one side of me. He rolled over and kissed his way down from my shoulder to one of my breasts.

"Let's not find out," Storm said. He was on the other side of Frost, his arm draped over his hip, hand hovering near his rapidly growing erection.

"Sounds like a good plan." Frost teased my nipple with the tip of his tongue before drawing my sensitive peak between his lips and sucking.

"I always have good plans," Storm said. He

wrapped his fist around Frost's length and pumped slowly.

"If your plan is to make me come in about three seconds flat, keep doing that," Frost said.

"Surprisingly, that's not my plan." Storm stroked him a couple more times before reaching for the lube and preparing Frost's rear hole for himself. Without dislodging Frost from my breast, he notched his cock into Frost's ass and slid into him.

Frost's eyes widened. "Fucking hell, that feels so good."

"Chelsea feels so good," Dallas said thrusting with deliberate slowness.

"They both feel so good," Storm said. Chances were, he was the only one currently in the room who'd find out, so no one could tell him he was wrong.

"I'm with Storm," Frost said, looking at my nipple. "Chelsea and I both feel incredible. Right, Chels?"

"Absolutely," I said. What else could I do but agree? I was feeling pretty damn good right then. "So you know, you all feel amazing inside me."

"Of course we do," Storm said. He pulled out of Frost slowly and with some reluctance, before handing him the lube. "Dallas, on your back so she's riding you. Chelsea lean forward."

We gave him the side eye, but did what he told us to. He clearly had something in mind. I was curious to see what it was.

My hands on Dallas' chest, I leaned forward as far as I could. Frost readied my rear hole with the lube and his fingers, before Storm gestured for him to straddle Dallas' legs behind me.

"Gladly," Frost said. He stroked his cock a couple of times before positioning himself and sliding into me.

I let out a long, low moan. If there was something I enjoyed, it was having as many of my guys inside me as I could take. If I could stop time, I'd stop it right there. Live in that moment forever.

If I did, I would have missed looking over my shoulder and seeing Storm position himself behind Frost and slide back into him.

"Holy fuck," Frost whispered. "This is..." He shook his head. He had no words for what this was. Honestly, neither did I.

Especially when Storm started to thrust, driving himself into Frost and pushing him deeper into me. In turn, rocking me onto Dallas.

Dallas' eyes widened. "I've never..."

"Neither have I," Frost said. "But I'm pretty sure this is what they mean when they say teamwork makes the dream work."

"Never say that again," Storm growled.

Frost chuckled. "I'm not wrong though, am I?"

"Definitely not wrong," I said, my eyes crossing with pleasure. "This is certainly a dream."

"It's not a dream," Storm assured me. He started to thrust more quickly, setting the rhythm for the rest of us. At the back of the pack, but completely in control. Just like he was out on the field. Exactly the way he liked it.

"Good, because I'd hate to be dreaming this," Frost said. "I'd like to put it on the menu and have it more often."

"Me too," I agreed. If we could find a way to include the other three guys, that would be even better. For now though, I was just going to enjoy this.

I rolled my hips in time with Dallas' and Frost's thrusts into me, savouring every second of having them both deep in my body. Knowing they must be tapping against each other every few strokes. Every so often, Frost would moan, confirming that.

Dallas just lay with his eyes closed, thrusting, smiling and enjoying every second.

"I could do this for days," Frost said. "Except for the fact I'm going to come very soon."

I responded with a half laugh. "Me too." I was right on the very edge of the precipice, my toes over the side. Ready to fall and fall and fall.

"Me three," Dallas whispered. "This is fucking incredible. Fucking...ahhh... Good." He thrust harder as he came at the same time I did. Our cries mingled like beautiful music. More beautiful still when Frost joined in a few moments later, quickly followed by Storm.

We were a choir of pleasure. Not in perfect harmony, but incredible nonetheless. Bonded by a love of football, orgasms and each other. If I could wake up this way every morning, I'd be a happy woman.

One by one, we flopped down side-by-side, all of us glistening with sweat but smiling.

"Wow," Frost said, trying to catch his breath. "Storm, when you get an idea, you get an idea."

"His head is big enough," Dallas remarked. When we all turned to look at him, he shrugged. "Atlas wasn't here to say it, so I figured I would."

"Don't make me tell you to fuck off," Storm said.

"I think we already got the fucking covered," I said, stifling a yawn with my fist.

"There's always room for more," Storm said. "Dallas didn't seem to be complaining."

"I wasn't," Dallas agreed. "If it'll make you feel better, I agree, it was a good idea."

"That does make me feel better," Storm said. He sucked in a breath before exhaling slowly. "To be honest, I've been thinking about it for ages. Now seemed like the right time to do it. You know, spur of the moment and all that."

Frost patted his bicep. "If you get any more ideas like that, I'm here for it. In the meantime, I need a shower. Let's get Chelsea cleaned up."

"Let's get you cleaned up too," Storm said, his expression softening. "Unless you need another reminder, I just came in your ass."

Frost grinned. "As if I could forget." He rolled over to straddle Storm and kiss him. After a moment, Storm wrapped his arms around him and kissed him back.

"While they're busy," Dallas whispered. He grabbed my hand and pulled me with him toward the ensuite bathroom.

"We know what you're doing, you know," Storm said before we slipped inside and turned on the shower.

"Nothing to feel guilty for," Dallas said before

closing and locking the door. He grinned and backed me into the shower, underneath the hot spray. He grabbed the body wash and started to clean me up, starting from my face and working his way down. He made sure to thoroughly clean my pussy and ass before washing one foot then the other.

Rising back to his feet, he grabbed the shampoo and cleaned my hair, rinsed it and applied conditioner.

"I don't know much about women's hair care products, but I know you need to leave that in for a couple of minutes," he said with a cheeky look in his eyes.

"Whatever shall we do for those couple of minutes?" I teased.

"It's my turn to have good ideas," he said. He pressed me back against the shower wall and hooked his hand under my thigh. Gripping my leg around his hip, he positioned his cock and slid into me again.

I'd never met a man who got so hard again so fast. Sometimes, it was all I could do to keep up with him. This morning, I was ready for round two as well.

I held on to him and tilted my head back so the conditioner didn't dribble into my eyes. My back under the warm water, I rolled my hips to meet his hungry thrusts.

"I've been thinking," he said between strokes. "Is there a way to become surgically attached to you?"

I laughed. "No, and you wouldn't want that anyway. You'd get stir crazy pretty fast."

"That's a risk I'm willing to take," he said. "Sometimes I wish I met you sooner. I would have whisk you away somewhere private before anyone else could see you or touch you. It would have just been you and me all night every night and forever."

"You don't like having the other guys around?" I asked, enjoying the way his cock rubbed against my clit as he thrust.

"I do, but I like having you to myself too," he said. "But you might not have liked it if you were only with me. I would have liked to be your first though. Was he good to you?"

I swallowed hard. "Um, yes, he was. He was very thoughtful, considerate and gentle."

I hoped he wouldn't press for any more information than that. The topic arose a couple of times, so to speak, but I'd managed to dodge it so far.

"Anyone I know?" he asked. The water poured down his face. He blinked and shook his head as it fell into his eyes, droplets clinging to his eyelashes.

He was so gorgeous it almost hurt. So sweet, loyal and loving. So protective, so willing to do anything for me. If he'd proven anything, he'd proven that, even to the potential detriment of his sanity.

"Someone you've met," I said. "But let's not talk about that. In fact, let's not talk at all." I squeezed my muscles as tight around him as I could, hoping to distract him from the conversation.

He groaned. "Not talking is good." He started to thrust faster now, pushing us both near and nearer to coming.

Not talking was very good, but I kept that thought to myself. Hopefully he wouldn't remember later and ask again. Some secrets were best kept private. Especially something like this. Besides, I didn't want to know who he fucked first. The only thing that mattered to me was who he fucked last and who he was fucking right now. Whose body he was grinding into as he cried out his second orgasm of the morning.

Once again, I came the same time he did, clutching onto him as the water washed over us, rinsing off sweat before it could cling to us. Our cries mingled with the steam in the bathroom.

"I fucking love you," he said mid-orgasm. His voice was ragged, but his words were clear. Like somehow in that moment he needed me to know.

Me saying it back was equally important. I

needed to do that as often as I could, with all of the guys. I needed them to know and I needed to remind them, just in case.

"I fucking love you too," I said, letting myself get lost in the bliss of his body against mine. Universes were born and exploded into a thousand tiny stars in those moments before I finally came back down to earth.

He slid out of me and wrapped me in his arms, holding me under the water while we both caught our breaths and our hearts slow, slick skin against slick skin.

We stayed like that for too long and yet not long enough before we finally pulled apart.

"Time to rinse your hair," he said. He turned me around under the water and started to do just that.

Chapter Sixteen

Jay

"Would you believe this is my first time in Fiji?" Chelsea pushed the strap of her laptop bag up her shoulder and stepped down off the plane beside me.

I glanced over to her and managed a slight smile. "I've lost count." We travel to so many places sometimes they all blurred together.

"I will too, soon enough," she said. "All of this flying around everywhere, do you get over it sometimes?"

"Are you asking as my doctor or my..." I glanced around to see who was listening. "Girlfriend?"

"Both," she said, after doing the same check.

"Yeah, sometimes." I adjusted my tie, certain this

time it was going to strangle me. Who invented these things anyway? And who decided we had to wear them? I would have been happier getting off the plane in jeans, a T-shirt and bare feet. Instead, we had to wear suits, like we were heading to the office.

"You know what I get over?" Frost asked from directly behind us. "The amount of times I've asked if we could go and lie on the beach and drink cocktails. They keep saying no."

"Poor baby," Storm said with no sympathy. "It's not like they pay us to play football or anything."

"They don't pay you to look pretty," Atlas told him.

"I'd give you the finger, but people are watching," Storm told him. "Pretend I'm doing it."

"No thanks," Atlas said. "I'll think about the other kind of fingering."

Storm snorted. "Not gonna happen."

Atlas shot him a look, mouth open, tongue out in mild, playful disgust. "Not from you."

"You're both spoilsports," Frost complained. "Right, Jay?"

"I guess so," I said, only half paying attention to them. How had we gone from Chelsea checking in on me to fingering in two minutes or less?

Okay, that was becoming the new normal pretty fast. If I was honest, I liked it. If nothing else, it deflected attention from me. The only thing I wanted to be in the middle of, was a bed, surrounded by naked lovers. Not the centre of attention at the airport.

"So they never gave you time off to drink cocktails?" Chelsea asked, reining in the conversation somewhat.

"They herd us back on the plane as soon as we finish playing and get changed," Frost said. "Sometimes I feel like a performing sheep."

"Is that even a thing?" Storm asked. "Performing sheep."

"It used to be," Frost deadpanned. "But then they used to fleece everyone."

Storm groaned and smacked his hand to his forehead. "I should have known that bullshit was coming. No wonder a guy drinks."

"Do you go to the baa for that?" Atlas grinned.

"Fuck off," Storm said. "Don't you start with the stupid puns."

"Buck off," Atlas replied. "I don't answer to ewe. In case you missed it, that's spelled E... W..."

"Yeah, I get it, dickhead," Storm snapped.

"Shear up," Frost said. "The puns aren't that baaad."

Storm rolled his eyes. "I'm starting to reconsider this relationsheep. I mean, relationship." He was struggling to hold back the smile that tugged at the corners of his mouth.

"You know you love me." Frost gave him a side on hug as they kept walking. "If we were at home we could go for a drive in your Lamb-orghini and spend some time together."

Storm stared at him. "I don't have a — fuck. All right, no more stupid sheep puns."

"Sheep live in pens," I said, trying to keep my expression as deadpan as Frost had.

"What Jay said," Atlas said. "Without them, they'd be running wild. That might be what Storm wants."

"You guys are out of your minds," Storm said.

"Which is exactly why you love us so much," Frost said. "We keep you entertained."

"That's one word for it," Storm grumbled. "If you're not careful, they won't let you through customs." He raised a finger and pointed at Frost. "Whatever sheep jokes you have, save it."

Frost raised his hands to either side in surrender.

"I was out of sheep jokes. If you're going to be in a moood, then —"

"Don't start with cow puns," Storm warned. He pulled out his passport as we entered the terminal, ready to show the local customs officers as we filed past.

"They keep things interesting, don't they?" Chelsea said to me softly as she stepped behind me in the line.

I grunted. "That's one way to put it. I guess they kinda make things easier. Lighten the mood and stuff, y'know?"

"It's true what they say about laughter being good for you," she said. "It relieves stress and makes people live longer. Even if they're only sheep puns."

"I'm surprised they didn't get to goat puns." I glanced over my shoulder at Ramsey.

He grimaced. "Don't remind them."

I smiled. I didn't think Frost needed too much reminding, but he wouldn't hear it from me.

I pulled out my own passport and opened it so it could be inspected and scanned. The team handled any other travel documentation we needed, so I knew everything would be in order. As expected, the officer handed back my passport and waved me through.

"They probably know all of you on sight," Chelsea said, pushing her own passport into her skirt pocket.

"It wouldn't surprise me," I said. "They even seem to know who I am."

"Of course they do," she said, walking beside me again. "You're just as important as any other player on the team."

"I guess, but I don't talk to the press much," I said. Knowing they might be waiting once we left the airport put me on edge. "They wouldn't know my face as well as the others'. They all know Storm, because he always has something to say. And Frost because he's friendly. And Dallas has his moments." I nodded to where he was walking in front of us.

"And they notice Atlas because he's Atlas." I was going to say he was smoking hot, but that was obvious. He was the kind of guy who drew gazes wherever he went. Even if people didn't know he played football, they stopped to stare. And me, I was just Jayden Lang, the guy from Western Sydney who happened to be good at rugby.

"They notice you too," she assured me. "Speaking of being noticed..."

We stepped out into the Fijian sunshine, only to

see a contingent of Australian press gathered around our bus.

"Storm, what can you tell us about the death of your head coach?" one shouted.

"Was it just an accident?" another yelled.

"Dallas, Frost, what can you tell us about the general manager, Bruce Fergus? Would you say it's a coincidence that he died, then Coach Stanley?"

"Would you say the Smashers are cursed?"

We pushed through them towards the bus, not answering any of the questions. The more they yelled, the higher my anxiety rose. My hands started to tingle and my heart raced.

"Jayden Lang, can you give us some words about Coach Stanley?"

I found a microphone shoved into my face, right in front of my nose. My first instinct was to grab it and throw it to the ground before stepping on it and crunching it into a million pieces.

Instead I muttered, "No comment."

"Come on, you must have something to say," the journalist insisted. "You're sad about it, right? Would you say you miss his leadership?"

With the palm of my hand, I shoved the microphone away and all but ran onto the bus and right down the back. I threw myself down onto a seat and curled up on myself.

"Jay?" Of course it was Atlas who approached me carefully, gesturing for everyone to give me some space. Chelsea wasn't far behind, looking worried, but also keeping a careful distance.

"Hey." Atlas eased the strap of my bag off my shoulder and handed the whole thing to Chelsea, who stashed it in the rack above us. "It's okay. They shouldn't have been up in your face like that." He looked like he might get back off the bus, grab the microphone and shove it down the journalist's throat.

"They just wanted to know how we were feeling," I said, half to myself.

Was that a bad thing? The team released statements, but people always wanted to know how the players felt at times like this. It wasn't unreasonable, was it? I hated that I felt like I overreacted. I hated that it got to me like this. They had microphones in everyone's faces and no one else ran off like I did.

"They were pushy and rude," Atlas said. "They should know better. You did nothing wrong."

"I should have kept my cool." Right now, I couldn't remember what my cool felt like. My heart was racing so hard. Taking a deep breath was a struggle. I wanted to curl up in a ball. At the same time, I wanted to scream at the whole world to fuck all the way off.

I wiped my eyes with the back of my hand. No way I was going to cry in front of my team. Fuck, why couldn't this happen at the hotel, or somewhere I could melt down in private?

"I barely kept mine." Atlas took my hands and squeezed them gently. "We're on the bus now. You won't have to deal with them again."

"But when we get to the hotel—" I started.

"They won't come near you," he promised.

Chelsea sat in the seat opposite, facing us. "We'll all make sure they don't." She shook her head, her ponytail flicking back and forth. "Is that normal? I haven't seen the press behave like that since I joined the team."

"It can be," Atlas said. "Especially when something goes down like losing two major people. It's bullshit; how do they expect us to feel? Of course we're going to be grieving. Of course we think it's fucked up. What did they want?"

"What do they ever want?" I asked. "They think if they push, we'll say something juicy." If I was worked up enough, I might. Or I might have punched one of them. That would make a great headline. For them, not for me. I'd be in a shit ton of trouble.

"Then they're out of luck, because we don't have anything juicy to tell them," Chelsea said with a faint smile.

"We have plenty, but we're not telling them." Atlas squeezed my hands again. "I'm sorry this happened. I should have been closer. I should have put myself between you and them." He looked frustrated at them and himself. As if somehow he let me down and not the other way around. The last thing I wanted was to behave in a way that embarrassed the team. I couldn't stay there anymore, listening to the barrage of questions. The overwhelm was too much to handle.

"You can't protect me forever," I said quietly. Sooner or later, he'd get sick of doing that, right? He'd start to feel overwhelmed and crowded. By me.

"The hell I can't," he said. "That's what I'm here for. To make sure you're good, no matter what goes down."

Frost popped up from the seat in front of us. He gave me his usual smile with no hint of judgement. If he thought I was some kind of emotional mess, he gave no sign. "He can and so can the rest of us. Right guys?"

"Right," Chelsea said firmly. She nodded at Frost to sit back down, giving me my space.

He flopped back down immediately.

"See, everyone gets it," Atlas said. "We've got you, because we love you." He let my hands go and reached for his seatbelt.

I fastened my own and turned my gaze towards the window to watch the scenery roll by as we made our way toward our hotel.

Chapter Seventeen

Chelsea

"How are you doing?" I asked Jay gently.

He looked pretty shaken up after the run in with the press. I tried to step in, but the journalist had all but shoved me out of the way to push the microphone into Jay's face. For a moment, I honestly thought he was going to punch the man. Instead, he quickly removed himself from the situation and found a quiet spot on the bus to deal with the rush of emotions.

Storm would have just punched the man in the face and worn the consequences. Atlas too, given half the chance.

We all knew what my brother would have done.

At least no one shot at any of us. This time.

If they were going to, that would have been the

perfect opportunity, while we were distracted. On the other hand, there was also a shit load of witnesses.

"Better," Jay said softly. "Thank you." He sat in the centre of the bed, stripped down to his underwear, squeezing a stress reliever toy that looked like an owl. From the look of it, it got lots of squeezing.

When we arrived at the hotel, we carefully arranged ourselves around him, forming a shield around Jay. Fortunately, only a few members of the press followed us from the airport, so the questions weren't as intense or loud. Still, we hurried inside and up to the room Atlas and Jay were sharing.

In theory, I had a room to myself. Right now, I wouldn't be anywhere but here unless Jay and Atlas didn't want me in the room. If that was the case, I'd respect their wishes. The last thing in the world I wanted to do was crowd Jay when he was struggling to calm himself.

"You don't have to thank us." Atlas sat on the side of the bed. He'd also stripped down, wearing only track pants. "Like I said, that's what we're here for."

"Exactly," I agreed. "If people don't understand personal space, then we'll remind them. Politely."

"I feel like Frost would pout if he heard you say

that," Atlas remarked. "He'd be disappointed he couldn't flay them or something."

I sighed. "Sometimes I feel like I created a monster. If he hadn't gotten involved with me—"

"He would still have found a way to let his darkness out," Atlas said firmly. "Some people can't help themselves. If they didn't find violence, it would find them. Look at Jay and me. We were both sweet and innocent once. Okay, Jay was."

Jay choked back a laugh. "I don't think I was even born sweet and innocent. Why bother when being dirty is more fun?"

"I could have said those exact words about myself," I said with a smile.

Growing up in Dusk Bay, I was never going to be innocent. Was I ever sweet? Maybe, but it was so long ago I couldn't remember. I'd started stripping and selling my body shortly after I started my first degree. My first paid fuck seemed like a lifetime ago.

He was tall, with brown eyes. Slender, like a runner, but with a cock like a horse. He knew exactly what he wanted, taking me from behind while I was on my hands and knees. He made it all seem so easy, instructing me on exactly how to give him what he wanted. Apart from that, he barely said a word. He just fucked me, climbed off and dressed again before sliding a wedding ring back onto his finger and leaving.

He came back a bunch of times, always asking for me, always fucking me without his ring, as though somehow he could pretend what he was doing wasn't cheating. I never knew his name and, after a year or two, he stopped turning up. Sometimes I wondered what happened to him and his wife. Given it was Dusk Bay, she probably found out and poisoned his coffee.

Shame, he was a good customer.

"You're very sweet," Atlas told me. "And beauti-ful." As he spoke, he undid the buttons of my blouse, one by one. "Gorgeous. Cute. Smart." He pushed the fabric of my shoulders and put it aside while Jay unhooked my bra.

"You're both of those things too," I said. "Espe-cially beautiful."

"I don't think anyone's called me beautiful before," Jay said.

"Fuck," Atlas swore. When we both turned to look at him, he grinned. "I knew I was forgetting something. Jay, you're beautiful."

"You might be shortsighted," Jay said. He pushed my bra off and let it drop to the side.

"Definitely not," Atlas said. He pushed me down

gently onto my back and undid my skirt before pulling it and my panties off. "I have an idea, if both of you are game."

"Is he actually asking permission?" I said, directing the question to Jay.

"He seems to be," Jay agreed.

Atlas narrowed his eyes at us before pushing his pants off and kicking them aside. "When you put it that way... Jay, get naked. I'm getting the lube." He helped off the bed and over to his open suitcase, returning a moment later with a tube in his hand. "We're going to need lots of this." He opened the lid.

My heart skipped a beat with anticipation of what he might be thinking. So far, none of them suggested anything I didn't want to do with enthusiasm. I suspected that would be the case now too.

"Jay, lie on your back," Atlas ordered. "Chelsea, you too. Spread your legs." He gestured for me to open them wide.

I lay down beside Jay and bent my knees, opening them so far my knees touched the bed covers.

"I love how fucking flexible you are." Atlas squirted some lube onto his fingers and smeared it around my already wet pussy. He squirted out more and slathered it all over Jay's cock, then more on his own.

"Chelsea, ride Jay's cock and lean forward as far as you can."

I glanced at Jay to make sure he was okay with this so soon after what happened at the airport. When he nodded eagerly, I straddled him, lowering myself down onto his cock.

"Lean forward a bit more," Atlas said. He straddled Jay's legs behind me and moved in close. "That's it." He pressed the head of his cock to my entrance, right beside Jay's.

"Have you ever taken two cocks in your pussy at the same time before?" Atlas asked. His voice was rough with need.

"Never," I said with some trepidation. Both of them were so big, they were going to stretch me to my limit. Could I do this? I was willing to try. I'd never backed down from a challenge yet; why start now?

"Good, because you're about to." Atlas pushed himself in a little more.

At first, my muscles tensed reflexively, trying to resist the extra pressure. I forced myself to relax and let him press in deeper still. Bit by bit, he eased himself until they were both all the way inside me.

"Holy shit," Jay whispered. "That feels so... Fucking... Incredible. I can feel both of you, like..." He shook his head, out of words to describe the way it felt.

"Amazing," I whispered. I'd felt full before, but never like this. Never with two thick cocks so deep inside me, pressed up against each other.

"Next level," Atlas agreed. Very slowly and very carefully, he started to move his hips back and forth, creating friction without letting himself fall back out.

"Why haven't we done this before?" Jay whispered.

"Because we didn't have Chelsea before," Atlas said. That was all the explanation he gave and none of us asked for anything more. Honestly, I couldn't have conjured too many coherent words anyway. This was like nothing I ever experienced before, and I'd experienced a lot.

As Frost would say, this was definitely something I wanted to put on the menu to do later. He and Storm would be down for it, as would Frost and Jay together. Would it feel different with different combinations of my guys? I looked forward to finding out.

"I'm going to come," Jay said, his voice strained.

"Me too," I said, just as strained.

"Yeah, me too," Atlas said, sounding slightly disappointed in himself. Of course, this was his first time doing this as well. With practice, we could hold out for longer. I'd happily fuck like this for hours. Or try to, anyway. With the pressure on my clit and all the way through me, keeping myself from coming might be a hell of a challenge. One I was happy to face head on. So to speak.

For now, I let myself go, tumbling over into the abyss, my muscles tightening further around both of them and making them both come, spilling themselves around each other. Filling my pussy to overflowing with their cum.

"I can feel...everything," Jay said, groaning out his orgasm. "I felt Atlas come."

"I felt you come," Atlas said, like it was some kind of revelation. It might have been. "I've fucked before, but now I dunno... It's like fucking both of you at the same time is... Epic."

"I know what you mean," I said. I thought I'd done pretty much everything I could do, but I was wrong. There was always more to do and more to learn. And more to enjoy.

I was one lucky girl.

As carefully as he'd fucked, Atlas eased out of me and flopped down beside Jay.

Tentative, because I was a little sore now, I rolled off Jay onto the other side of him. For a while, I lay on my back and stared at the ceiling.

"Thank you," I said after a few minutes.

"For what?" Atlas asked.

"For being you. Both of you," I said. "For being sweet and adventurous."

Atlas propped himself up on his elbow and looked over at me. "You were expecting us to be vanilla?"

I snorted. "Of course not, but looks can be deceiving. You could have preferred the missionary position with the lights off."

Atlas burst out laughing and Jay not long after.

"I'm not sure if I should be insulted or not," Atlas said between laughs. "For one thing, I've never fucked with the lights off. At least, not in total darkness. I like to see the person I'm screwing."

"I have," Jay said softly. "Because I didn't want to be seen, not because I didn't want to see. Then I met Atlas and he never made me feel like I needed to hide."

"You don't need to hide," I assured him. "Not unless you want to. You're gorgeous and your body is incredible. You have nothing to be ashamed of. Nothing at all."

Like Atlas, I'd never screwed in the dark either. At Flirts, the rooms were dimly lit, not dark. For safety reasons, they were always illuminated. Not to mention client preference.

When I wasn't fucking for money, I liked to see my partner and I liked to be seen. And I loved what Atlas did for Jay's self-esteem.

They really were adorable together. If I wasn't head over heels for both of them, I'd fall here and now. As it was, I fell a little deeper. I never wanted to get out.

With any luck, we had years in front of us.

"I love you both," Jay whispered, breaking the comfortable silence.

"We love you too," Atlas replied.

"Yes, we do," I agreed. "We should get cleaned up and go down for dinner."

"I'm only going down there if we can come back up and do this again," Jay said.

I rolled over to face him. "Deal. The sooner we get down there, the sooner we get back."

We all jumped up from the bed and raced to the shower.

Chapter Eighteen

Chelsea

"You look serious." I slid into the chair opposite Doctor Stuart and placed my hands in my lap. "Is everything all right?"

He sighed. "This is the part of my job I dislike the most."

My heart sank. That sounded ominous. I tried hard to keep myself from being too distracted, but the last few days were particularly challenging. We'd been back and forth from Fiji, then Brisbane. The guys won both games, but the second by only a narrow margin. The stress was starting to take its toll.

I glanced down at the desk. "Please just rip the Band-Aid off." If he was going to fire me, he might as well spit it out and we could get on with our lives. It would save us both the pain of a drawn out conversation.

He chuckled.

I looked up at him and frowned.

"I have to evaluate all new staff members after a couple of months with the team," he said with a cheeky smile. "I hate doing it. If you've done anything I don't like, or don't agree with, I would have told you by now."

He bobbed his head back and forth. "But management insists I make this an official interview. Which is why I didn't tell you about it in advance. This nonsense is stressful for everyone."

"You scared the daylights out of me," I said dryly. "Does this mean you're not going to fire me?"

"Fire you?" he scoffed. "Of course not. You're doing an excellent job. I apologise. I couldn't resist playing this up a little bit. When you get to my age, you'll take your laughs where you can get them."

I shook my head at him, but managed a smile. Any other day, I might have found it hilarious. Considering the pressure I was under, seeing the funny side was more difficult.

"Unfortunately, we still have to go through the list of things I needed to consider when making my evaluation." He rolled his eyes wearily, opened his laptop and turned it so we could both see the screen.

"As you can see, I've left positive comments for each item, along with some constructive feedback on aspects you can still continue to work on. For the record, I have areas I still need to work on myself. This is by no means a condemnation."

"I understand that," I said. "We never stop learning. There's always going to be more to know."

He was absolutely right when he mentioned I could learn more about the players' mental health and the impact the game had on it. Especially after Jay's meltdown in Fiji.

This was an area we hadn't covered at university. Not to the extent I considered necessary, anyway. That was something we could all work on more.

"Me too," he agreed. "I've made a particular note about your relationship with the players. I have spoken to several of them about you and they all adore you. Some of them even went as far as to say they'd prefer to be treated by you." He sniffed, but his expression was playful. "Apparently I'm not cute enough."

I snorted. "You're definitely cute enough. It's their loss if they don't agree." He was adorable in that trustworthy, older man way. Like a kind uncle.

He laughed. "That's sweet of you to say, but we both know I'm far from cute. So you know, I reminded them your ability to treat them wasn't based on how you look. Some of them are still back in the dark ages. They're getting there, slowly. Some more than others. Have you had any trouble with any of them?"

"Not really," I said. Most of them wouldn't dare, given the response they'd get from my boyfriends if they tried to harass me. And for those who were familiar with Dusk Bay, from my brother. Sometimes, having a brother who could make people disappear was an asset. The threat of that alone would keep their mouth closed and their hands well away from my ass.

"They've been welcoming," I added. "Their families have as well, when I attended the family clinic. I think a lot of the wives like having a female doctor they can see if they want to."

Doctor Stuart nodded. "Of course, I'm all about women making those sorts of choices. In my day, it would have been laughed at. You know what they say, we've seen it all before. Patient comfort wasn't the consideration it is now. Fortunately, the world and medicine has come a long way from that malarkey. To be honest, that was one of the reasons I wanted you to work here. I do my best to make my patients feel comfortable, but that's not always possible."

His expression turned slightly grim. "Some of my colleagues from back in the day would have shaken their heads. They were certain they knew best and all they needed, or wanted, to do was get on with the job. Most of them have retired now, or work in administrative duties."

"Or lecture at university," I said flatly. "We had one or two of those when I was there. Doctor Chance, for one. He always seemed to mark our work harder if we were women."

I didn't mind having my work carefully scrutinised, but not because of what was between my legs. What mattered was what was in my brain.

Doctor Stuart grunted. "Ah yes, George Chance. One of my contemporaries. He was always certain men were superior to women, for some reason. Personally, I've always thought the opposite was true."

"I like to think we're equal and what's more important is how we treat each other," I said.

I didn't miss university and I certainly didn't miss Doctor Chance. He'd retire soon and the medical program would be better for it.

"Two hundred percent," Doctor Stuart agreed. "My wife would be with you on that. She's always saying people could be nicer to each other. You never know when folk might pass on." His gaze dropped and he exhaled deeply.

It didn't take a genius to know he was thinking of Bruce Fergus and Max Stanley. The team had lost a couple of basically decent men. Even though he wouldn't have hired me because of my past as a stripper, Bruce Fergus wasn't a bad person as far as I was concerned. Not really.

Coach Stanley was one of the good ones too. The team was definitely missing his absence.

"You really don't," I whispered. "Life is fragile." Especially when people went around firing guns near me, and *at* me.

For all I knew, I could be dead tomorrow, and all my guys with me. My heart ached at the idea. I wanted to grow old with all of them and do all the things we dreamt and planned. Maybe have children someday. With six fathers, they'd be loved. Honestly, they'd probably be spoilt rotten, but they'd grow up to be good people. How could they not with all the good role models around them?

He cleared his throat. "Very much so. Which is exactly why I'm contemplating my own retirement.

Not this season, but maybe next." He turned his laptop around and closed it. "It's time I travelled with my wife and not a bunch of football players." He smiled. "We don't know how much time we have left; I don't want to waste a minute of it."

"You deserve to have a rest after how hard you've worked," I said. "The team is going to miss you like crazy though. I hope we can hold the place together when you're not around anymore."

He snorted. "I'm quite sure the place won't fall apart if I leave. But it's very nice of you to suggest it might. I'll certainly feel lost when I'm not here. My wife might well send me back to work after the first week, when I get on her nerves from boredom." He steepled his fingers and placed them on the desk top.

"I'm sure she'll be thrilled to have you at home more often," I assured him. No doubt there'd be a transition period, but they'd work through it. "I'm guessing you'll be here for every home game anyway. It'll be like you never left."

He smiled. "I absolutely will. I won't miss a single game. I might even travel for some of the away games. The team can always use an extra voice to cheer them on."

"Phew." I swiped a hand over my brow. "For a

minute there, I thought you were going to admit you wanted to cheer for someone else."

He barked a laugh. "Never! Once a Dusk Bay Smashers man, always a Dusk Bay Smashers man. Supporting them is in my blood."

"Mine too," I said. "I might even try to save you a seat on the plane when they play away games. Someone needs to keep the guys in line while we're flying."

"I was going to hand that job to you," he said pointedly. "I trust you can give them a kick up the bum when they need one. Tell them it came from me."

I laughed. "I can absolutely do that." The team wasn't going to be the same without him around.

While he was still here, I'd learn as much from him as I could, but I'd miss him more than I could express. He'd always been so kind to me. Sometimes I felt it was more than I deserved. "It's going to be difficult to replace you."

He scoffed. "If they don't offer the position to you or Otis Skinner, I'll be surprised."

"I don't think I'd have the experience," I said. "Unless you stay around for another five or so seasons." As for Skinner, he had to still be alive.

I mean, so did I, but I wasn't the one trying to take on the Brantley family. Whatever he was up to could get both of us killed. I preferred it to be him than me.

"There's more to consider than experience," he said, as though reading my mind. Of course, he didn't mean it in the way I was thinking, but I appreciated the vote of confidence.

"I guess we'll see," I said. "Either way, I'm glad to be able to work here. In whatever capacity that might be."

"The team is lucky to have you," he said. "It won't be long before other teams are trying to poach you. I've already spoken about you to a couple of my peers. Don't be surprised if they come poking around. I've already told them you won't leave, but that's unlikely to stop them."

My face heated. "That's sweet of you. You never know, they might come up with an amazing offer I can't refuse." Since it was unlikely they'd let me take six players along with me, I wouldn't even consider it.

"I'm sure they'll try," he said. "You may even want to take them up on it. No one would blame you if you did. You'd learn a lot from whoever you end up working with."

"It sounds like you're trying to encourage me to apply for jobs elsewhere," I said.

"Not at all." He picked up a pen and started to turn it around with his fingers. "All I'm saying is that you should keep your options open. Nothing more."

"I'll keep that in mind," I said. "Was there anything else you wanted to talk to me about?"

"No," he replied. He glanced at his watch, an old analog one. "You have a session in the pool with some of the players, I believe?"

"Yes, I do," I said. I was actually getting in the water with them today, and learning more about aqua therapy. If it wasn't for Otis Skinner, I'd be excited for it.

Instead, I was nervous as hell.

Chapter Nineteen

Chelsea

I IGNORED THE LOOKS AS I STEPPED DOWN carefully into the warm water. I was used to men staring at me like that. Admiring my body. Often when wearing a lot less than a swimsuit.

As long as they continued to behave professionally, it didn't bother me to have them look. Besides, I knew none of them would try anything anyway. Even if I wasn't involved with so many of the men on the team, there were other staff here, including Doctor Skinner.

"Mr Ramsey has kindly agreed to let you sit in on his session," Skinner was saying. "He's been working on easing minor knee discomfort and the levels of anxiety that come with playing sports at a professional level."

I reached the bottom of the shallow pool and bobbed over to Ramsey.

"Thanks for letting me watch," I said softly.

He leaned in and whispered. "Always happy to get wet with you."

I smiled and whispered back, "Don't be inappropriate with a member of the medical team."

"Nothing inappropriate. You're my girlfriend." He straightened up as Skinner looked at both of us, eyes narrowed.

"As I was saying," Skinner continued, "you're all familiar with the traditional types of aqua therapy. Using the water as resistance while taking the pressure off muscles. The benefits on players' mental health is something I know we're all passionate about."

He looked around those gathered, as though daring them to disagree with him. Of course, no one did. Nor would they.

Instead, we agreed, vocalising with a murmur that passed through the handful of people gathered.

Skinner nodded to me and bobbed to the other side of Ramsey. "We're going to put out our arms and Mr Ramsey will lie back, letting us support him in the water." He nodded to both of us.

I held out my arms, mimicking him, while Ramsey relaxed, floating on his back.

"This is nice," Ramsey said.

"Close your eyes," Skinner said.

Ramsey did as he was asked.

At the same time, a shiver passed through me. It would be all too easy for Skinner to press a hand down on Ramsey's face, pushing him under the water. If the people gathered around us were working for Skinner and King, they might make no move to stop him. They might even help, because I sure as hell had no intention of standing here and letting him kill one of my boyfriends.

"Is there a problem, Doctor Miller?" Skinner asked.

My eyes snapped to him. "Of course not. I was thinking how nice it would be to have nets to lie on in the water. Something that would support weight, and allow the players to do this if there aren't others present."

I wasn't thinking that, but I gave myself a pat on the back for coming up with it on the fly.

"I like that idea," Ramsey said before Skinner could respond. "This is good too." He kept his eyes closed the whole time.

"Indeed," Skinner said. "However, that is not the

point of this therapy. Doctor Miller, kneel down in the water and place your arm under his neck. Take hold of his opposite arm, as you might if bathing a baby."

I knelt and did as he asked, while he stepped back from us. I was supporting Ramsey now, while the rest of his body floated gently.

"Good, now swivel your upper body and arm in the water, taking him slowly in a semicircle around you," Skinner directed.

Careful to keep my grip, I did as he asked, moving Ramsey slowly all the way to my left, then back all the way to my right.

"This is nice," Ramsey said. The sides of his mouth twitched upward.

"Shhh, relax," Skinner told him. "Let the motion be the only thing in your mind."

The sides of Ramsey's mouth twitched again, but he pressed his lips together and relaxed a little more on my arm.

"Good, now remove your hand from his arm and support him only with yours," Skinner directed.

I glanced at him for a moment, but did as he instructed. I wasn't able to move Ramsey as much, and I had to go slower, but I guided him with a small amount of touch while still keeping his head out of the water.

Thankfully it was him I was doing this with. I suspected Jay wouldn't like it, and the others would resist giving up control. Except for Dallas. He'd be all for it. Frost too, if he could stop making jokes and laughing.

"Now, don't stop your movements," Skinner said. "Place one hand on his shoulder and let the opposite rest under one knee."

Without losing rhythm, I followed his instructions, supporting Ramsey's leg while his other dropped deeper under the water.

I didn't know about his mental health, but this was doing wonders for mine. The movement was almost hypnotic and the water deliciously warm.

Was there room at our new house to add a pool like this? We could all take turns practising the Watsu method on each other. Not to mention all the other aqua therapy methods people had developed. We might even develop some of our own.

"Very good," Skinner said. "Now place your arm under both his knees. Then bring them up slowly towards his face and down again."

I felt like I was holding a large, muscular baby, but Ramsey was so relaxed by now, he gave me no resistance. Still, a few of these would be good exercise for me.

"Combine the rotation with this accordion technique," Skinner said. "Start slowly, it may take time to coordinate the movements."

He wasn't wrong there. I had to focus on folding and unfolding Ramsey before I could go back to swishing him slowly back and forth. I hadn't realised aqua therapy took quite so much concentration. We might both fall asleep after this.

"Don't lose your rhythm," Skinner said. "Get your accordion movements more accurate, rather than the rotation. You don't need to rush. This isn't the dance floor."

I managed a smile while forcing myself to concentrate harder. This was definitely going to take some practice, but I could definitely see the benefit of it. This would be a fabulous way to de-stress.

We continued like that for a few minutes before Doctor Skinner stepped in to take over and demonstrate some more complicated techniques.

I watched carefully, following his movements like I was still supporting someone.

Fortunately for everyone, he made no attempt to drown Ramsey or anyone else.

After about twenty minutes, he nudged Ramsey's

legs down toward the bottom of the pool and stepped away from him.

"I trust you feel less tense than when you entered the water?"

"If I was any more relaxed, I'd fall asleep." Ramsey knelt in the water and rolled his shoulders. "Not gonna lie, I thought that was weird to start with. But it was good. I'd do it again. Thanks."

"It looks like I need to do some more studying so I can be certified to do that myself," I said.

I didn't mind one bit; I loved learning. And the obvious boost to Skinner's ego was clear to see. This time, we didn't have to fake being on his side. I'd love to learn more of this and all the other techniques. A person couldn't know too much.

"I'm happy to give you recommendations," Skinner said. "Aquatic therapy is the future."

Why did he have to be on the wrong side? I could learn a ton from him, and I'd be happy to do it. And work closely with him, to include more and more players in this program. That would be so much nicer than thinking he wanted to kill us, or knowing there may come a day where we'd have to kill him.

Right now, that seemed like both a million miles away and a waste.

"I'll do more," Ramsey said. "I'll tell the other guys too. Storm might loosen up after a session like that."

That was hopeful, but I was willing to try. We could even work up to Storm and Atlas supporting each other's weight in the water. That would be the ultimate test of trust.

"The whole team would benefit," Skinner said. "You may go." He nodded to both of us before moving away as a couple of other players stepped into the pool to run laps down the lane on one side.

Ramsey's eyebrows twitched up at the curt dismissal, but he didn't say anything. Instead, he placed his hand on my lower back and led me to the steps and out of the pool.

"That was nice." He lowered his hand, but the look on his face suggested if we weren't surrounded by people, he'd peel the swimsuit off me and fuck me here and now. The front of his board shorts was tented slightly, his erection getting the better of him for a few moments.

"Yeah, it was," I agreed. I stepped over to pick up my towel and wrap it around myself. "It's nice to forget about things for a while. Just enjoy the water and all that. They could do with piping some music in here though."

He grinned. "Some loud rock would be just right."

I snorted. "I was thinking something along the lines of classical music or ballads, not rock, but whatever floats your...body."

"I really would fall asleep then." He snatched up his own towel and dried his face. "I need something loud to keep me awake."

"There is that, I suppose. Storm or Atlas would probably prefer something loud too."

I couldn't quite imagine either of them floating to the sounds of Mozart or Beethoven. On the other hand, it wouldn't hurt either of them to try. They might decide they liked it.

"I better go and get changed and get back to the infirmary," I said. "I have a few appointments this afternoon."

"I'm going to hit the gym," Ramsey said.

I frowned at him. "Haven't you worked out already?" He did a workout at home before coming here for training, then did another workout in the pool before the relaxation therapy session. Now he wanted to exercise again? I was starting to worry about the extent he was overdoing it.

"I still have energy to burn off," he said, but his eyes were averted.

"Ramsey—" I started.

"I'm okay," he said before I could get very far. "I just like to work out, okay?"

One hand holding my towel closed, I held up the other in a conciliatory gesture. "All right. Just don't overdo it, or you risk injuring yourself." I knew he knew that, but he had me concerned and I had to say something.

"I won't," he assured me. He lowered his voice and added, "I love you."

"I love you too." I gave him a quick kiss on the cheek and a smile before he hurried off to do another round of exercise. I didn't know how he had the energy after relaxing for as long as he had. I'd be ready for a nap.

I watched Otis Skinner work for a while longer before slipping out of the pool area.

The moment the cooler air hit my skin, I was snapped back to alert. Like it or not, Skinner was the enemy and I had to be careful. Especially when two people were shot in my proximity.

I'd do whatever I could to prevent a third.

Chapter Twenty

Chelsea

I PULLED MY CAR INTO THE HUGE GARAGE AND closed the door behind me when my phone rang. I'd like to say I have a cool ringtone, like a Taylor Swift song or something from Wolf Venom, but it was just one of the phone's built-in sounds. One of these days, I'd get around to changing it to something better.

I glanced over to where it lay on the seat beside me as Sadie's name flashed up on the screen. I picked it up and put it to my ear while getting out of the car and closing the garage door behind me.

"Hey." I leaned against the car while I pulled off my shoes. "How are things?" I unlocked the internal door and stepped into the house. Dropping my shoes and bag beside the door, I walked to the kitchen to turn on the kettle for a cup of coffee.

Judging by the cars in the garage, and the sound from elsewhere in the house, most of the guys were home. The only car that seemed to be absent was Ramsey's. The other guys tended to travel back and forth from the stadium together, when their schedules aligned.

Ramsey often had other things he needed to do outside of football. Things I tried not to ask too much about.

"Not bad," she said. "I'm feeling a lot better. My gunshot wound doesn't hurt anymore."

I winced, but I knew she was saying that to sound badass. Not everyone could claim to have an injury, or scar inflicted by a bullet, and live to tell about it. Personally, it wasn't the kind of scar I coveted, but each to their own.

"That's good," I said. I held the phone in place carefully with one hand and pulled a mug out of the cabinet, along with coffee and sugar. "I'm sure you'll have an impressive scar."

"That's the hope." I could hear the smile in her voice. "What's the point of getting shot if you can't brag about it?"

"I'm sure I don't know," I said with an edge of sarcasm. "I would have preferred it not happen at all."

"Yeah, well, you've got to take the good with the bad. How's things there?"

"Pretty good," I said. "It's been...almost a week since anyone in my proximity was shot."

She laughed. "Things are looking up, then?"

"For now they are." I slid open a drawer in the massive island and pulled out a spoon before scooping coffee and sugar into my cup.

I had to step away from the kitchen while the kettle boiled. Even when they weren't loud, I always had a problem hearing past them. It was a sensory problem that fortunately didn't impact my life too much. Just when I was trying to make coffee and talk on the phone at the same time.

"Maybe everything that was going to happen has happened," she said. "That might be it. You know what things are like. Sometimes someone quietly takes care of a problem and we don't hear about it for a long time afterwards."

"That's true," I conceded.

I was a long way down the proverbial food chain. If the Brantley family had Nyla Fox executed, it was unlikely anyone would bother to let me know. It could be weeks before they deigned to tell Ramsey, if they did at all. Although, if she was ultimately behind this, we would have seen some change in King and Skinner's behaviour. Wouldn't we?

From what I'd seen, they were as calm and controlled as ever. And neither of them had pulled any of us aside to suggest we join them in any kind of retaliation.

No, I decided she was still alive. As much as I'd like to hope we were, we weren't out of the woods yet.

"You don't think it's safe to come back yet, do you?" she asked sadly.

"I wish I could say it was, but I don't think so," I said. "I'm not sure when it will be, if ever. Is life away from Dusk Bay so bad?"

I was teasing gently, but it was a serious question. She might be better off not coming back at all. Even if we survived this situation, there'd always be another, and another after that. If it wasn't the Crimson Vipers, it might be the Brotherhood of Kings pulling some shit. Or someone else who wanted to rival the Brantley family. Or maybe the Brantley family themselves flexing their muscles. Or...

The list was endless. She might be safer where she was.

"I miss you and I miss working," she said. "It's

nice to spend time with my parents, but I'm starting to remember why I moved away. They still think of me as their little girl. If they knew exactly the kind of club I work in, they'd be horrified. Which I still can't get my head around, because it's only nudity and sex. But they're old-fashioned. If they had their way, I'd have nothing in my wardrobe but long skirts and turtlenecks."

I pictured her rolling her eyes.

"I can't imagine you in a turtleneck," I said. The kettle clicked off and I stepped back into the kitchen to pour the hot water.

"Me either," she said with a laugh. "I'd feel like I was being choked, but not in a good way. Although, it would be handy to hide bruises from a hand neck-lace. Maybe I'll invest in one or two, just in case."

Trust her to think of an advantage to wearing something like that. Maybe that was why they were invented in the first place. They looked cute on a lot of women, but she wasn't one of them; neither was I. Like her, the only things I wanted around my neck was a hand I could trust, or a nice, warm scarf.

"You might need enough for a week if you're covering bruises," I teased. "Does that mean you've met someone?"

"I might have," she said evasively. "It's early yet, but I like them a lot."

"I'm happy for you," I said sincerely. "Are you sure you want to come back here then? They might not want to come with you."

"I think they will," she said. "I know I said it's early, but they care about me a lot already. I think if I return to Dusk Bay, so will they. But I won't make any choices until it's safe. Putting myself at risk is one thing, I won't risk them too."

"It sounds like love to me," I said, again half-teasing.

"It might be. I've never met anyone like them."

I could picture her blushing as she responded. "Awww, that's adorable. I've never heard you talk about anyone like that. Do they have a name?"

"Darcy," she replied. "Don't start singing Sadie and Darcy sitting in a tree."

I laughed. "I wouldn't dare. I'm just happy you're happy. You deserve it." I placed the kettle down and picked up the end of the spoon to stir my coffee.

"You deserve it too," she said. "You sound settled."

"I am settled," I said. "Apart from the threat of violence hanging over us. I have the job of my dreams and six amazing boyfriends. What more could a girl want?"

"Judging by the sound of the spoon, coffee that isn't instant," she teased.

"Ha ha," I replied. "We haven't gotten around to getting a fancy coffee machine yet, okay? You know what I always say, instant coffee is better than murder."

"I've never heard you say that," she said.

"Now you have," I said with a laugh. "Although, most things are better than murder."

I didn't think my brother would agree with me. Frost might not either. Or Atlas. The others, they'd do what they had to.

Although, I wasn't sure if Dallas was capable of taking another life. Killing India was hanging around his neck like the proverbial albatross. Haunting him. Made worse by seeing Sierra killed.

"That depends on the instant coffee," Sadie joked. "Some of it is so bad, I'd have to refute your statement."

She didn't mean that literally. At least, I didn't think she did. We knew most of each other's secrets, but not all of them. For all I knew, she might secretly be an assassin. At this point, I wouldn't be surprised if she was.

Except, would she have left Dusk Bay if that was the case? She might have if she was ordered to go. If that was the case, she wouldn't be able to tell me anyway, so I didn't ask. Besides, if she did tell me, she might have to kill me.

Some secrets were better kept secret.

"I miss you," I said. "It's nice to have another woman to talk to once in a while."

"Testosterone overload, hmmm?" She laughed. "We should have anticipated that might be a problem."

"It's not a problem," I protested. "It's just nice to have a female friend to giggle with and talk about stuff the guys aren't interested in. Like the colour of my toe nail polish."

"Who says I'm not interested in the colour of your toe nail polish?" Frost said as he stepped into the kitchen. He glanced down at my bare toes, then up at my face before wiggling his eyebrows at me. "We could paint our toenails together."

"You're both missing the point," I said, assuming Sadie heard what he said through the phone. "I just mean women have a different perspective on things, that's all. Once in a while a girl likes to have some girl time."

"I mean, if Sadie wants to move in, I'm happy to watch." Frost grinned. "Or I could join in." He reached for a glass before holding it under the tap to fill it with water.

"Sadie isn't moving in," I said. "And if she was, I'm not interested in her like that. And vice versa. Sorry, you'll have to settle for watching me with the other guys instead."

"I'm down with that." He toasted me with his glass before gulping back the water.

"I thought you might be." I tossed my teaspoon in the dishwasher before taking a sip of coffee. "Anyway, where were we?"

"You were telling me you were missing me," she said. "I miss you too. It's nice to hear your voice. I'm happy that you're happy and I hope everything works out the way you want it to."

"Me too," I said. "I hope it'll be safe for you to return some day. And that Darcy takes good care of you."

"They will," she assured me. "They know what's good for them. Now, if you'll excuse me, I have to go and shop for turtlenecks."

Once again, I laughed, then said my goodbyes and ended the call.

"You really do miss her, don't you?" Frost rested his hip against the island.

"It's not that you guys aren't enough," I said quickly.

"I get it," he said. "If there were six women and me in this house, I'd probably want a dude to talk to once in a while. Which gives me an idea. Do you trust me?"

I gave him the side eye but said, "Of course I do."

"Then let me arrange something. I promise you'll love it."

I didn't know what he had in mind, but he had me intrigued.

Chapter Twenty One

Chelsea

I PEELED BACK THE CURTAINS AND LOOKED OUT as moving light framed the window.

The big gates at the front of the house stood open. A dark car slowly moved through, toward the house. A couple of moments later another followed.

We finished dinner and packed the dishes into the dishwasher. I was just about to settle down and watch TV with the guys.

Instead, a shiver of fear travelled up my spine.

Anyone showing up at this time of night couldn't be good.

I turned around. "Who—" I caught the look on Frost's face and stopped, my mouth still open. "What did you do?"

His grin widened. "You'll see."

Storm stepped over to drape an arm over my shoulders. "Don't worry, he had a good idea for once."

"Hey!" Frost protested. "I have lots of good ideas."

"Of course you do." Jay gave him a side hug. After a moment, he added a quick swipe of his lips over Frost's.

"I knew you had good taste," Frost told him.

"Of course he does," Atlas said, looking smug.

Storm snorted loudly. "You would think that. For some reason, he digs you."

"He digs me because I'm awesome." Atlas shrugged. "I can't help it, I was born that way."

"Who told you that?" Storm asked. "Your mother? She's biased."

"That doesn't mean it's not true." Atlas was sticking to his guns, but grinning the whole time.

"Of course it's true," Jay said. "Chelsea chose us, so we must all be awesome."

"Exactly." Frost nodded. "I'll get the door."

His arm around Jay's waist, he walked over to the massive front door and unlocked it. He swung it open just as Daisy Lasalle got out of her car in front of the house. Mina DiMarco climbed out of the car behind hers.

"What is this?" I whispered, only loud enough for Storm to hear.

"Frosty figured you could use some other women to talk to," Storm said. "Who else is going to understand what you're going through?"

Tears threatened to slide down my cheeks. I blinked them away. "That's really thoughtful."

He was right too. If anyone was going to comprehend the way I was feeling about...well, everything, and how overwhelmed I was, it was these two women. They'd each been through the fire and walked away, their heads held high.

"Yeah, Frosty has his moments," Storm said softly.

I glanced over to see him watching his boyfriend, looking at him with the same expression of love he had in his eyes when he looked at me.

"You both do," I whispered.

Storm looked over at me and smiled. "Yeah, well, don't tell anyone. People might start to think I'm nice or something."

"We wouldn't want that," I teased.

"Definitely not." He nodded. "I have a badass asshole reputation to maintain. I don't want anyone or anything to compromise that." He gave me a wink.

I leaned into him and inhaled the heady, masculine scent of the man. He'd changed a lot since we met, softening around the edges when he was around us. He too, had his moments, but he'd also found his place in the world, in our little family.

"Welcome!" Frost held the door open for both women to step inside.

"Chelsea." Daze greeted me like I was a long lost friend. "You're looking well." She waited until Storm moved aside, to give me a hug.

"You too," I said, with only slightly less enthusiasm. I reminded myself that either of these women could have me killed if they wanted to. If they were here as friends, I'd treat them like that.

For now.

"Mina," I said politely. She wasn't given to hugging, so I didn't offer one.

She seemed to take in every millimetre of her surroundings, as if assessing the place for threats and escape routes. After maybe half a minute, she nodded to herself, then to me.

"Frost said you were feeling isolated." Daze walked over to the sitting room and made herself comfortable, while the guys dispersed to other parts of the house.

Ramsey, I noticed, headed to the gym.

I sat down near Daze. Far enough to face her and keep an eye on her, but close enough to be friendly.

"I'm used to being surrounded by women," I

started. "Now I'm surrounded by men. And watching my back everywhere I go."

"Women can be dangerous too." Mina sat on an armchair, her hands in her lap. She always had an air about her, like a cat ready to use her claws.

I never saw her be anything other than cool and calm, but I had no doubt she could inflict damage before I could blink. Anyone who underestimated her was out of their minds.

"Ain't that the truth?" Daze laughed. She crossed her legs at her knees and leaned back. "There's, what? Six men in this house? But I'd be willing to bet the three most dangerous people in this building are the three of us."

I gave a slight cock of my head. "I don't see myself as dangerous." Not compared to them especially.

"Why not?" Mina asked, scrutinising me without blinking.

"I —" I wanted to shrivel under her gaze, but I managed to keep my back straight.

"You know how to use a gun and a knife?" Daze asked. "You know how to use your brain, and your body. With your medical knowledge, I bet you know more ways to inflict damage than most people. Not necessarily kill them, but incapacitate them."

"I guess so," I said reluctantly. "I mean, I do, but could I actually do it?"

"Of course you could," Mina said bluntly. "If you're up against a wall, or in a corner, you will. You won't even think about it. You'll act." She seemed certain of that.

"I'm scared I'll panic," I said in a small voice.

"Is that what's held you back all these years?" Daze asked. "You're scared to be who you were meant to be because you're worried you're not up to it?"

I pressed my lips together. "I'm not sure this is what I'm meant to be. I just wanted to be normal."

The expression on Daze's face was sympathetic. "I thought I wanted that too, for a long time. I took my daughter and I out of Dusk Bay for years, hoping to put the place behind us."

"What happened?" I asked.

"I came back," she said. "I came back and I realised this is home. This is who I am and who I was meant to be. As soon as I embraced that, I've never looked back."

"I was also...away," Mina said softly. "But this was always my life too. We can deny it all we want, but this is us. Besides, we can't leave the men to run things. They'll make a mess."

I bit back a smile. Did she just accuse Reuben Brantley of incompetence? Judging by the hint of humour in her eyes, this was her idea of a joke. Of course it was; he was anything but incompetent. Only she'd get away with saying anything like that. Anyone else would be dead before the sun rose. Or wishing they were dead.

"Things certainly work out better with us to keep an eye on them," Daze agreed. She cocked her head at me. "What else is holding you back?" She wasn't pulling any punches tonight.

"People keep shooting other people in my vicinity," I said. "It feels like...I don't know, the deeper I get involved, the more the people I care about are put at risk."

"That comes with the territory," Daze said, but not dismissively. "Especially when you're in the position you are right now. Working for us, but having to play nice with the enemy. Getting caught in the middle is inevitable. But you've done well. From what I gather, King and Skinner trust you."

"As much as they trust anyone," I said. I glanced over to the door. "They didn't—"

"No one saw us come here," Mina said. "We wouldn't risk you like that."

Of course they wouldn't, they still needed me.

Like a chef needed their favourite paring knife. Or a racehorse owner needed their best mare.

Daze must have seen my expression and knew what I was thinking. She moved over closer and put a hand over mine.

"This isn't just about what you can do for us, Chelsea. I like you. I always have. I'm ecstatic to have you back in the fold, even if you're not. I'll be just as relieved as you are when this is over and you can get on with things. What Mina meant when she said we wouldn't put you at risk was exactly right. Not just because of your position with the team, but because you're you. Okay?"

I swallowed back a knot of emotion. "Okay."

"Daze is right," Mina said. "You're a valuable part of this organisation. If you wanted to, you could go a long way. You could be as powerful as we are."

"But not more so," Daze said with a laugh.

Mina raised her eyebrows at the other woman. "I thought that was implied."

Daze grinned. "I was just saying, that's all."

"I figured that was the case," I said. I was never going to be more powerful than Reuben Brantley's girlfriend, or Daisy Lasalle, who was one of his right hands.

Could I really be like them? Did I want to be?

Maybe they were right, and this was me. My place in the world. My destiny. What would happen if I stopped fighting it?

Mina sat forward, hands on her thighs. "What you said about the people around you being vulnerable. The more powerful you are, the less vulnerable they become. The easier it is to protect them and be protected by them. Yes, you accumulate enemies here and there, but it's a lot easier to have them dealt with."

She seemed to be remembering something from her past, something very satisfying. I presumed a woman like her would have enemies, but apparently they were taken care of.

"I don't know if I want to accumulate enemies," I said.

"Ramsey told me what happened to you and your friend, Sadie," Daze said. "It seems to me, whether you like it or not, you already have. Do you want to sit by and wait for them to come at you again, or do you want to get to them before they get to you?"

"Before they get your boyfriends," Mina added.

I looked down towards the coffee table. "I don't want anything bad to happen to any of them."

"Then you have your answer." Daze sat back. "Are you ready to take your place as one of us?"

I swiped my tongue over my lips. I considered the question and all the ways I could possibly answer. In the end, there was really only one. The only thing that would keep me and my men safe.

I looked up to both of them.

"Yes."

Chapter Twenty-Two

Jay

I hung back with Frost while the women were deep in conversation. I couldn't hear what they were saying, but Chelsea gradually relaxed in their presence and seemed to enjoy herself. Dallas took them in wine and snacks before retreating back with us. Satisfied they were okay and had everything they needed, we headed into the other sitting room to watch a movie. Or half-watch, because I wasn't interested in classic movies about giant killer sharks. I liked the real thing and hated the perception they were all out to eat every human they encountered. But the rest of the guys wanted to watch, so I sat with them and scrolled on my phone.

Just as the movie was ending, Daze and Mina left.

I was about to find Chelsea when she found us.

"Hey." Dallas grabbed her hand and pulled her into his lap. "How did that go?"

She nestled into him. "It went well. I have to admit, it was nice to have some girl time for a while. Thank you, Frosty."

Frost grinned. "Any time. It's good to see you smiling."

I turned the sound down on the TV and tossed the remote aside. "Yeah, it is. I guess that was what you needed."

If it was anyone but Frost or Atlas, I might have felt a pinch of envy for not thinking of it myself. Instead, I was happy for her. She deserved to have all of her needs met. If we couldn't do it, then she needed people who could.

Collectively, we were a lot of things, but none of us were women. If she needed girl time once in a while, I was one hundred percent behind it. Fuck knew we got plenty of guy time.

"It was," Chelsea agreed. "For lots of reasons." She shook her head slightly. "What were you guys watching?"

"Some shark movie," I said.

I'd tuned out after the first ten minutes, keeping most of my attention on the doorway and wondering what the women were talking about. The rest of my attention was on the close proximity of Frost. I was becoming as attached to him as I was to Chelsea and Atlas. It was hard not to like the outgoing prop.

"It doesn't sound like I missed much," she said.

"You didn't," Dallas said. "I missed you." He buried his face in her hair.

I was surprised he managed to stay in here with us, not right beside Chelsea. Being as far as several metres apart must have been borderline painful for him. It wasn't easy for me either, but I didn't feel the need to be glued to the way he was.

Not that I judged him. I liked the guy. He got to feel however he wanted to feel. Just like I did.

"I missed you too." She wrapped her arms around him and squeezed.

"Did you talk about cocks?" Frost asked.

I gave him a look.

"What?" He grinned. "Isn't that what women talk about when they get together? I mean, what else is there to talk about?"

"Pussies," Dallas said without looking up.

Chelsea laughed. "No, we didn't talk about cocks. Just between us, I don't want to think about Reuben Brantley's cock."

"Good," Dallas said. "You can think about mine."

"I think about yours a lot," she assured him.

"And mine?" Frost asked.

"And yours," she agreed. "And Jay's. And Storm's. And Atlas'. And Ramsey's."

"But no one else's?" I asked.

Was I feeling insecure? Maybe a little bit. She had six boyfriends. She might want a seventh or an eighth. If she did, I wouldn't stop her. If those men could give her something we couldn't, I'd accept that. But sharing her with five others was plenty for me.

"Definitely no one else's," she assured me. "I'm a six cock girl."

I couldn't help being relieved. I knew it showed on my face. "I'm a two cocks and one pussy guy."

"Me too," Frost said, giving me a smile.

"You know where I stand," Dallas said. He started to undo the button of Chelsea's jeans and work them down her hips. She'd barely kicked them and her panties off before he had the waistband of his track pants pushed down and lowered her onto his erection.

"I feel like it's been days," he murmured.

It couldn't have been more than hours, but no one corrected him. If I was honest, I couldn't get enough of her either. None of us could. I knew what everyone was thinking right now, it was clear from their body language. The question was, who was going to move first?

In the end, it was Storm who had his pants shoved down to his thighs, erection in his hand before he pressed the head between Chelsea's lips.

"Jay, come over here," Atlas said. He gestured for me to kneel down in front of him. He too had his pants down and his cock out. He placed his hand on the back of my neck and guided my face down to him.

I ran the tip of my tongue around his head a few times, teasing him before taking him into my mouth.

At the same time, Frost knelt beside me, waited until I nodded that it was okay and worked my track pants down until he could wrap his hand around my cock.

I shivered at the warmth of his touch, his broad hands stroking me, pumping me. Cradling Atlas' balls in my hand, I sucked harder, letting him fuck my mouth until I gagged. Just the way we both liked it. I slipped my other hand down the front of Frost's pants and around his length, pulling him out and working him the way he was working me.

I lifted my mouth from Atlas and leaned down to take Frost into my mouth, all the way down to my throat.

Frost moaned and straightened up a little, enough to place his own mouth on Atlas' cock.

Atlas placed his hand on the back of Frost's head, holding him there, fucking his mouth slowly, deliberately until he came, spilling his release into Frost's mouth. He thrust in a handful more times before sliding himself out. "I want to see you suck each other," he said.

Frost and I exchanged glances before lying down on the rug, cocks in front of each other. We both gripped each other's lengths in one hand, balls and the other and resumed sucking.

He tasted so good, I could have sucked for days. Not to mention, the guy had a magic mouth. With every suck, I rolled my hips, bucking against him, increasing the friction.

"You guys are perfect," Atlas said. "Make each other come."

As if he flipped a switch, I couldn't hold myself back if I wanted to. I fucked Frost's mouth harder and faster as he did the same to mine. A heartbeat after him, I came. My balls tightening before releasing down his throat and taking a mouthful of his.

I looked over to Atlas as I swallowed down every

drop. Frost waited until I was looking before he did the same with my cum.

He smacked his lips. "Delicious."

"You too," I said, suddenly feeling shy.

We were all distracted then by Chelsea coming loudly, her breasts bouncing as she rode Dallas. He came right after, his eyes squeezed shut with concentration, losing himself inside her. Storm was right behind, then Ramsey, who'd stayed in the corner of the couch, his hand on his cock. He watched all of us fucking while he got himself off. He didn't seem to mind it a bit.

I certainly hadn't. I was starting to realise I didn't mind being watched, if it was one of these six incredible people.

My family.

Chapter Twenty Three

Chelsea

"When you're finished there, Dominic King wants to see you," Doctor Stuart said as he stepped into the infirmary.

I looked over from my laptop. "Do you know what it's about?"

He shook his head. "I have no idea, sorry."

I frowned, but finished typing and pressed enter before grabbing my phone and slipping out of my seat. "I guess I'll be back shortly." I waited until he nodded his acknowledgement before hurrying out the door towards the elevators.

I sent a quick text off to the group chat to let the guys know where I was going. I wasn't alone in the corridor or the elevators, so they should have nothing to worry about. Neither should I, but I was sweating by the time I reached the GM's office.

I smiled at his PA, who gave me a look before jerking her head back towards his door. "He's waiting for you."

I was sure that wasn't as ominous as it seemed. At least, I hope it wasn't.

I stepped into his office and forced a smile on my face. "You wanted to see me?"

He looked up from his computer, sat back and crossed his arms. "Have you seen the news this morning?"

My heart skipped. "No, I haven't. Is there anything I should—"

Without another word, he turned the computer around until I could see the headline on the screen.

My heart sank.

"Stripper works as doctor for Dusk Bay Smashers."

The exact headline I dreaded for a long time. So long, I started to believe I wasn't going to see it after all. The team respected me and so did my colleagues. I truly thought I'd found my place here, and the past was where it belonged, in the past.

I should have known better than to be so naïve.

"You know I don't work there anymore," I said softly. We'd had this conversation when he started here. He didn't care what I used to do, as long as I was dedicated to the team. Or to whatever his agenda was.

He turned the computer back around and steepled his fingers. "It doesn't matter. It is now public knowledge and it's making the team look bad. People are questioning whether or not I knew about you. I've denied it, of course."

"Of course." I wouldn't expect him to act any different. Whatever happened, he had to cover his own ass. In his position, I would have done the same thing.

"That doesn't change the fact that it isn't a good look for the team. We're supposed to be an example to children. To society. We're people who work hard and play hard, but are held to a certain standard. This does not meet that standard." He looked at me down his nose.

"I can see how it might raise eyebrows and cause complications," I said carefully. "But what I used to do shouldn't—"

"It does," he said. "Regardless of what I may or may not think about your former profession, I'm put in an uncompromising position."

Fuck.

I swallowed hard. "What are you saying?"

"Your employment is terminated immediately. Please gather your belongings and leave the stadium." His voice was ice cold.

I swallowed back tears, but nodded. It sucked, but he was right. He had no other option. If he didn't fire me, it would look bad for the whole team. The reputation of the Smashers was going to take a hit as it was. This was the kind of scrutiny every club dreaded. I'd be public enemy number one with the fan base for a long time to come.

"I understand," I managed to say. "Thank you for letting me work here. It was an honour."

I started to turn away.

"Miss Miller," he said.

I noticed his intentional lack of my title, but turned back. "Yes?" He wasn't my boss anymore, I didn't need to refer to him as sir. I could think of a few other things I could call him, but none were appropriate right now. Not when he could just as easily have me killed if he wanted to.

"I will be calling on you to continue with your other duties for me." His eyebrows dipped, trusting I knew what he was implying.

I understood, loud and clear.

Just because I didn't work for the team didn't mean I wasn't working for him and Skinner, and

Nyla Fox. I felt like I was standing in the middle of a pile of quicksand, rapidly sinking deeper than I ever would have thought was possible.

"I understand, sir." Apparently that was warranted after all. "I'll, um, be ready."

"Of course you will." His eyes returned to his computer, dismissing me.

Struggling to keep myself together, I hurried out the door to collect my things.

No one was in the infirmary when I grabbed my bag and laptop. That was a small mercy I was grateful for.

No doubt Doctor Stuart would find out soon enough what happened to me. I would have liked the chance to say goodbye, but I wouldn't have been able to look him in the eyes anyway.

What would he think when he found out what I used to do? That someone like me had worked so closely beside him? I suspected he'd be disappointed in me and in himself for not realising. For thinking I was better than I was.

It was best he wasn't here to witness my walk of shame.

I sent off another text to the guys to quickly explain what happened. No doubt the press would want to talk to them. I didn't want any of them blind-sided. Jay in particular didn't need a surprise confrontation with a microphone. Not because of me. That would come, but I trusted the other guys to look out for him. And each other. They were all going to be pissed off.

I didn't look anyone in the eyes as I took the elevator down to the ground floor and hurried out the side door of the building. People stopped to stare, but I kept my gaze averted.

Whatever judgement might have been visible on their faces, I didn't want to know. None of that mattered now. The only thing that did was to get out of here as quickly as I could.

Stepping out into the sunshine was a relief, but it was short lived.

I made it half a dozen steps, heels clicking on the concrete, before someone grabbed me from behind.

Dark fabric was draped over my face and I was jerked off my feet. Thick arms wound around me, holding me hard.

I tried to scream, but a hand was firmly clamped over my mouth. I struggled against them, but they were too strong. My frantic kicks failed to connect.

As if I weighed nothing, I was thrown into what felt like the back of a car, landing so hard I cried out.

Put the pain aside, I told myself. *Focus.*

I needed to get up, to run. Rule number one, never let them take you to another location. If that happened...

Before I could move, a boot was closed over me with a thud. Total darkness surrounded me. The tang of grease and oil mixed with something metallic. Blood?

Don't freak out, don't freak out, I told myself. Only years of training in keeping calm stopped me from losing my shit. Just barely.

I barely managed a squeak of surprise and fear before the engine revved and the car drove away from the stadium.

Thank you for reading! The final instalment of the story is Deadly Ruck! Please leave a review if you enjoyed this book.

If you love a bonus scene of the guys setting up a sex room in the basement, you can get that here.

About the Author

Maggie Alabaster writes reverse harem romance.

She lives in NSW, Australia with one spouse, two daughters, one dog, and countless birds.

Shop direct from Maggie! Store

Sign up for Maggie's newsletter! Sign Up!

Join Maggie's reader group! Join here!

Follow Maggie on Bookbub! Click here to follow me!

Check out Maggie's website- www.maggiealabaster.com

Also by Maggie Alabaster

Aurora Hollow duet

Take Me Slowly Part 1

Take Me Slowly Part 2

Ruck Boys

Filthy Ruck

Hard Ruck

Twisted Ruck

Bad Ruck

Dirty Ruck

Deadly Ruck

Sparrow and the Mafia Kings

Possessive

Ruined

Corrupted

Pucking Dark Hearts

Pucking Hearts Collide

Pucking Forbidden Hearts

Pucking Hardened Hearts

Dusk Bay Demons

Puck Drop

Breakaway

Power Play

Brutal Academy

Book 1 Heartless

Book 2 Cruel

Book 3 Vengeful

Court of Blood and Binding

Book 1 Song of Scent and Magic

Book 2 Crown of Mist and Heat

Book 3 Sword of Balm and Shadow

Book 4 Whisper of Frost and Flame

Dark Masque

Book 1 Bait

Book 2 Prey

Book 3 Trap

Saving Abbie

Book 1 Pitch

Book 2 Pound

Book 3 Session

Book 4 Muse

Book 5 Rhythm

Book 6 Encore

Novella Venomous

Saving Abbie books 1-4

Saving Abbie books 4-6 + Venomous

Ruthless Claws

Book 1 Ivory

Book 2 Crimson

Book 3 Elodie

Harmony's Magic

Book 1 Summoned by Fire

Book 2 Summoned by Fate

Book 3 Summoned by Desire

Shifter's Vault

Book 1 Discarded

Book 2 Deceived

Book 3 Disgraced

My Alien Mates

Book 1 Star Warriors

Book 2 Star Defenders

Book 3 Star Protectors

Academy of Modern Magic

Book 1 Digital Magic

Book 2 Virtual Magic

Book 3 Logical Magic

Complete Collection

Summer's Harem

Book 1: Shimmer

Book 2: Glimmer

Book 3: Flicker

Complete collection

Short reads

Taken by the Snowmen

Jingle All the Way

Also by Maggie Alabaster and Erin Yoshikawa

Caught by the Tide

Book 1–Pursued by Shadows

Book 2 Pursued by Darkness

Book 3 Pursued by Monsters

www.ingramcontent.com/pod-product-compliance
Lightning Source LLC
Chambersburg PA
CBHW030021200726
48283CB00012B/710